HONOR BOUND

CANADIAN CHILDREN'S SERIES

The Canadian Children's Classics Series
from Quarry Press
presents books
of exceptional literary and cultural value
which have been written for children
by Canadian authors.

HONOR BOUND

Mary Alice and John Downie

ILLUSTRATED BY
Wesley W. Bates

[signature] 1996

Quarry Press

Honor Bound was first published by Oxford University Press in 1971.
A curriculum guide is available for this book from the publisher.

The publisher acknowledges the assistance of the Canada Council
and the Ontario Arts Council in the production of this book.

Canadian Cataloguing in Publication Data
Downie, Mary Alice, 1934
Honour Bound

(Canadian children's classics)
New ed.
Originally publ.: Toronto: Oxford University Press,
1971.
Includes bibliographical references.
ISBN 1-55082-026-5 (bound)—ISBN 1-55082-027-3 (pbk.)

1. United Empire Loyalists—Juvenile fiction.
2. Canada—History—1763–1791—Juvenile fiction.
I. Downie, John   II. Bates, Wesley W.   III. Title.
IV. Series.

PS8557.O85H6 1991 jC813'.54 C91-090443-X
PZ7.D759.D7592H0 1991

Design by Keith Abraham.
Typography by Attic Typesetting, Inc.
Printed and Bound in Canada by Hignell Printing, Winnipeg,
Manitoba.

Published by Quarry Press, Inc., P.O. Box 1061, Kingston, Ontario
K7L 4Y5 and P.O. Box 348, Clayton, New York 13648.

Contents

Prologue 7

1 June 1784   9
2 Departure   15
3 Papa's Adventures   23
4 The Lonesome Unicorn   31
5 Arrival in Albany   41
6 Alf Brown   47
7 Oswego   57
8 Cataraqui   65
9 Grimble's Plot   77
10 Supper With the Tricks   85
11 Visitors   93
12 Sam Talks 103
13 The Prophecy 113
14 Sam's Secret 129
15 Christmas Day 139
16 Miles Digs 149
17 Soot and Snuff 157
18 The Thieving Magpie 167
19 Alf's Visit 173
20 The Rapids 183
21 Honor Found 189
22 Miles Makes His Choice 201

Afterword 209
Further Reading 215

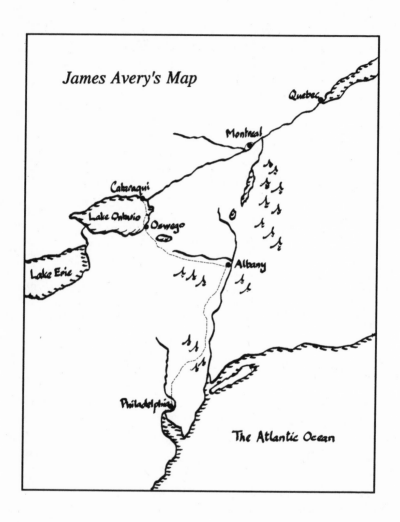

James Avery's Map

Quebec

Montreal

Cataraqui

Lake Ontario

Oswego

Lake Erie

Albany

Philadelphia

The Atlantic Ocean

Prologue

In the 1770s a family named Avery lived in a tall brick house in Quince Alley in the city of Philadelphia. James Avery taught Latin, Greek, and Mathematics to unwilling schoolboys during the day and at night he played the flute and argued about politics with his friends in a neighbouring coffee house. His wife Abigail looked after the house, the garden, and the three children: Honor, Miles, and Patience.

When the war broke out between the American colonies and Britain, the busy, secure life of the Averys came to an end. Unlike his neighbours, James Avery did not think that America should break away from Britain to become independent. He joined the Pennsylvania Loyalists and left Philadelphia to fight for King George. Abigail Avery stayed with the children, enduring the hostility of once-friendly neighbours.

During his first months in the army James Avery wrote often, but one day his regiment was shipped south. His last letter came from Pensacola, a Spanish town in Florida that was then in British hands. As time passed Abigail's friends tried to persuade her that he must be dead and that she should seek refuge behind British lines in New York, but she remained stubbornly convinced that he would come back. Even in 1783, while their neighbours rejoiced in victory, she and the children still did not lose hope of his safe return.

1

June 1784

"Look alive, there!"

Miles Avery sat up with a start and stared down from the brick garden wall where he had been dozing. Below him stood an old farmer wearing a flat black hat. A bag was slung over his shoulder and a crate of chickens sat at his feet.

"If you're going to lie on top of walls like a cat then you should be as alert as a cat."

Miles glared down suspiciously at the whiskered face.

"Do the Averys live here?" asked the rough-voiced old man.

"Yes."

"Open the gate, then. I have chickens to deliver."

Miles dropped to the grass inside the garden and opened the iron gate. The chickens squawked and fluttered as the farmer clumsily bumped the crate against it. When Miles turned around after closing and bolting the gate, he was surprised to see that the old man had already reached the door of the house. Without pausing, he pulled it open and went inside.

Miles raced after him and burst into the kitchen. The crate of chickens stood on the table and the bag lay on the floor, but the farmer was nowhere to be seen.

Miles ran into the hall to shout a warning to Mama and Patience, but a hand clamped over his mouth and he was swept off his feet into a bearlike grip.

"Hush, Miles," a familiar voice whispered. "I don't want to startle your mother. I've been away a long time."

Miles hardly heard him. He was staring in disbelief at the floor. There in a heap on top of the farmer's coat and hat were the whiskers and a wig of long grey hair. Miles jerked around.

"Papa!"

"Yes, it's me, Miles. I'm back."

The old stooped farmer was now straight and tall. His head was covered with long fair hair just like Miles' own.

"But—"

"Quick, go and get your mother and sisters."

"Miles?" Mama called from the staircase. "What are you doing down there? Have you been in another fight with Charlie Silas?" With a rustle of skirts she swept down the stairs into the hall, followed by Patience. "If you have been...James!"

"Papa!"

Their shouts of joy rattled the windows and the house came alive.

Mama and Patience fought to hug and kiss Papa. They laughed and cried at the same time until Patience developed hiccups and had to be patted on the back until she stopped. Embarrassed by this display of emotion, Miles ran into the study for his father's favourite pipe.

"Thank you, Miles," said Papa, walking after him, closely attended by Mama and Patience. "You have a long memory." He gazed around the room. "Many times I've closed my eyes and imagined being back here." He tapped the barometer with his pipe as he spoke, and spun the globe beside his desk. The room was quiet. He took a book from the desk and ran his finger over the smooth leather cover. The clock above the fireplace whirred and chimed five. With a happy sigh Papa sank into the big chair as his family clustered around him.

"I can't believe you're really here," said Mama. "Where have you been?"

"I'll tell you about that later."

"You'll never go away again, will you?" said Patience, holding firmly to his coat.

Papa laughed. "Sooner than you think. But now, to make my family and my homecoming complete, where is Honor?"

"She's in Albany helping Sally with her new baby," said Mama. "I know she's young and the times are dangerous, but Sally needed help badly and Loyalists have few friends left."

"The times could hardly be worse," said Papa. "I've been north, south, east, and west. Everything is in disorder, and any Loyalists left are making their way out of the country as best they can, in disguise and in secret. We are all under threat of banishment. Our properties are being confiscated, and anyone mad enough to stay will probably finish at the end of a rope. I'm sorry Honor is not here. Never mind—she can join us."

"What do you mean, James?" asked Mama.

"Are we going to England?" asked Patience.

"No."

"Where then?" asked Miles.

"Cataraqui." Papa walked over to the globe and turned it to North America.

"We are here now," he said, pointing to Philadelphia. Using the long stem of his clay pipe as a pointer, he traced a path north along the Hudson Valley to Albany, west along the Mohawk to the Great Lakes, and north again across Lake Ontario to Canada.

"Canada!" said Mama. "But that's a wilderness. Our only neighbours will be owls and wolves and wildcats. I thought we could go to England and civilization."

"The British government is giving land in Canada to those who fought for the King. We are poor now, Abby, and this will give us the chance we need to mend our fortunes. Life in England offers little comfort to the poor."

"But you're a schoolmaster, not a farmer," said Mama.

"Since I left Philadelphia I've had to try my hand at both soldiering and fur-trapping," Papa said lightly. "After that I positively look forward to the tranquil life of a farmer."

"What shall we do about Honor?" asked Miles.

"We will go to Albany and get her and we will try to persuade your aunt and uncle and cousins to come with us to Canada," said Papa.

"Will we live in the woods and eat nuts and berries?" Patience asked.

Papa laughed. "We will have to live in the woods, but not entirely on nuts and berries. Our crops will dazzle your eyes. And, when did you ever object to eating berries?"

Mama still looked unconvinced. "When do we leave?" she said uncertainly.

"Tonight!"

"Tonight? Impossible!"

"Tomorrow might be too late. One of our neighbours may already have recognized me and even the rumour of my return could collect a mob. I have seen others tarred and feathered and it is not going to happen to us!"

"But it will take at least a night to get ready," said Mama, pacing nervously about the room. "I can't pack everything in such a short time."

Papa gently but firmly sat her in a chair. "The cruel truth, Abby, is that there is little packing to be done. We'll take only what we can carry. The rest we must leave to looters. Do we still have the horses?"

"Yes," said Mama. "We rent them out when we can. The money helps us to buy food for all of us—that and my sewing."

"The horses will be a godsend," said Papa. "But remember, they must carry the four of us and our supplies, so pack only your most treasured possessions." He was interrupted by indignant clucking sounds coming from the kitchen.

"What's that?" said Patience.

"Chickens," said Papa. "I did not come back to you totally empty-handed. We'll cook one for super and take the other with us, to eat on the way. Now work quickly. We leave after the last watch. Put everything you want to take on the kitchen table and I'll stuff what I can in the saddlebags."

"Can I take Grandfather Dawe's sword?" asked Miles.

"*Small* treasures, lad."

"I'll take his pistol, then," said Miles. "My slingshot, fowling-piece, and jackknife will be useful too. I suppose I must leave my stuffed owl."

"I can't part with Father's clock," said Mama.

"I'll take Honor's dollhouse," began Patience. "She gave it to me for keeps when she went to Albany."

"Idiots all," groaned Papa. "I see that I must inspect your belonging like a customs man. Scamper off and prepare for the trip now, you packrats."

2

Departure

Miles went up to his room after supper and tried to decide what he should take with him on the journey. He looked around at the maps on the wall, at the long table littered with model cannons and soldiers, at the collection of small pots of chemicals beside a flask and burner at the far end of the room, then to the top of the old bookcase where a great horned owl stared at him through unblinking glass eyes. He took his grandfather's long sword from its place of honour on the wall over the regimental flag and pistol.

"I wonder if I'll ever be able to become a cavalry officer like Grandfather," Miles thought. "It won't be easy. I don't suppose I'll need a sword in the woods, but Grandfather wouldn't think much of me if I left it here for the rebels. If I could hide it, Colonel Miles Avery might come back some day and fetch it."

As he laid the sword carefully on the table the finely chased handle knocked over one of the toy soldiers. Miles set it back in position—it had been on guard duty—and became engrossed in the mock battle he had been conducting that morning. A cannonball had torn a gaping hole in the ranks of the rebel army and sent bodies flying in all directions. The rebels were in retreat. Now the cavalry charged. Miles moved a troop of his prized Philadelphia Light Dragoons across the table through the devastated ranks of the American army. "If the British and Provincials had fought that way," he thought, "we wouldn't have lost the war."

He undressed, blew out his candle, and got into bed. The moonlight lit a patch of ceiling where one of his chemicals had once exploded and splattered an interesting black pattern on the white plaster.

"If that were the plan of an enemy fort, I'd attack from the south." His eyes traced a wandering crack off to the corner of the ceiling. "And I'd bring in supplies along that road." A cloud passed over the moon and the road and the room disappeared in the darkness. Miles shifted restlessly on the hard narrow bed. His mind had been invaded by conflicting thoughts.

"I won't be sorry to leave Philadelphia and its 'patriotic' citizens. And now Papa's back, Mama won't cry at night when she thinks we can't hear her.

"I won't be sorry to leave Charlie Silas and his gang either. What will they do without Patience to chase and me to beat up?" Miles' face hardened in the darkness at the memory of his arch-enemy. "But I hate to think of those Silases looting my room. I must get even with them for making our lives so miserable."

"Eleven o'clock and all's well on a fine clear night!" cried the watch in the distance as he passed through the sleeping streets.

"I know what I'll do!" Drowsily Miles made his plans to

startle Charlie Silas. The watch cried again, strangely loud and close at hand this time. Suddenly Miles heard many voices. They came from a mob and sounded shrill and angry. He could see a barrel of tar standing by the gate. The mob was going to tar and feather Papa! Nehemiah Grubbs, the cooper, and all the neighbours were there. Charlie Silas and his brothers hovered, grinning, by the tar. Then, with a hoot of laughter, Charlie produced Grandpa Dawe's sword from behind his back. He thrust it into the bubbling pot and began to stir the hot tar.

"Here comes a few more feathers," growled the cooper and the crowd laughed as Cockatoo, Miles' pet rooster, came staggering across the garden, drunk from eating love-apples that had fermented in the sun. With a hoarse cry Grubbs seized Cockatoo by the neck and held him up to the crowd.

"Cockatoo!" bellowed Miles. He hurled himself at the cooper...and crashed to the floor fighting wildly with his blanket.

"What is all the hubbub?" Papa called from his bedroom.

"What is it, Miles?" The candle in Mama's hand cast a comforting glow before her as she came into the room.

"I had a nightmare," he said shamefaced, picking himself up from the floor and wrapping himself in his blanket again.

"With all the excitement today, it's not surprising," said Mama. "It is time to get up anyway."

"Already? I just went to sleep."

"You've been asleep for four hours. That's all the time we have for sleep tonight. Now get dressed."

Miles put on his clothes and rolled up his blanket. Then he took down the flag and pistol from the wall, stuck the pistol in his kit bag, and wrapped the sword in the flag. He took his fowling-piece from the corner and slung it over his shoulder.

He picked up the blanket, kit bag, and flag-shrouded sword and went to Patience's room.

Patience was dressed and sitting on her bag looking sadly around the room—at the bed with its high canopy like a fleecy white tent, at the chest with its brass handles that gleamed in the dark, at Honor's old doll's house, and at her half-empty bookcase.

"I don't want to leave anything behind," Patience said. "Everything will be broken or stolen."

"Don't think about it any more. Go downstairs. I'm going to hide Grandfather's sword in the chestnut tree and then I'm going to leave Charlie Silas something to remember us by. If Papa asks for me tell him I'm just finishing packing."

He went to the open window and looked out. "Make sure no one closes this!" Then, with the ease of long practice, he slid over the edge.

Patience stepped over to the window after him. Miles was moving rapidly across the roof like a cat. He dropped lightly onto the shed and disappeared in the darkness.

Patience picked up her bag, took a long last look around the room, closed the door, and went downstairs. A flickering candle in the hall sent a huge shadow chasing down after her.

Mama had set out bowls of hot porridge in the kitchen. "Where is Miles?" she asked.

"He'll be down soon."

"I'll take your bag out and saddle the horses," said Papa. He picked it up and set it down quickly. "Are you carrying bricks to Canada?" He opened to bag. "Books, books, more books, and no clothes at all!"

"I packed an extra bonnet at the bottom," Patience said.

"It's all right, James. I thought this would happen," said Mama. "I put some of her clothes with mine."

Papa shook his head and left to prepare the horses.

Patience ate her porridge slowly while Mama moved quickly about the kitchen, trying to decide what to pack. She took a large pewter platter down from the wall, considered it, and reluctantly put it back.

"It's useless," she said to Patience. "How can I know what we'll need in the woods?"

"Papa said the government will give us supplies," Patience reminded her.

"But not brass candlesticks or damask tablecloths," Mama said mournfully. Suddenly she brightened. "My silver spoons won't take much space." She began to stuff them hastily into a bag.

Papa came back into the kitchen. "The horses are saddled and ready; the last watch will pass shortly and then we can leave. Do you have everything Abby?"

"Not quite." She went to the study, followed by Papa and Patience. Her expression was determined. "I may have to abandon my feather beds and all my china to the rebels," she said, "but I'm not leaving Grandfather Dawe's clock to the thieving wretches!"

"That's madness, Abby! We're about to travel hundreds of miles through forests and unknown dangers and you want to take a clock."

"If the clock stays, I stay," said Mama. She sat down.

Papa heaved a sigh. "Very well, we'll take your beloved clock. But no more heirlooms, I beg you."

He picked up the clock. "Patience, run upstairs and bring the quilt from your bed to protect it. Tell Miles that he must come immediately. We leave in a few minutes."

Patience ran upstairs and leaned out of the window. The moonlight wandered over empty gardens—there was no sign of Miles. She heard the last watch call: "Four o'clock and all's well!" The cry sounded hollow and sad in the distance.

"Patience! Miles! Come at once. We are leaving."

She took the quilt from the bed and slowly walked out of the room and down the stairs.

"Where is Miles?" asked Papa impatiently.

"He is—" She heard a thud in the bedroom. At last! "He's coming," she said.

"What *have* you been doing?" Mama said to Miles, who had appeared at the top of the stairs red-faced and puffing.

"Sleepyhead!" Patience interrupted.

"Take your gear out to the horses," Papa said. "Patience, go with Miles. I'll bring the clock."

"Where were you?" whispered Patience.

"You'll soon see," said Miles. He followed Patience into the shed, where the horses, Robin and Richard, placidly munched hay.

Papa came into the shed with the clock wrapped in the quilt and tied it to a saddlebag.

"You will ride with Mama on Richard," he told Miles, "and you and I, Miss Bookworm, will ride together on Robin." He lifted Patience onto Robin's broad warm back. "Now if only your mother would come..."

As if she had heard him, Mama appeared. She was carrying a bag filled with strange bumps and bulges. "This is all, truly," she said before Papa could protest.

He helped her onto Richard's back while Miles opened the shed door, trying to keep it from squeaking. They led the horses into the garden, through the gate, out to the silent alley. Papa had muffled the horses' hooves with sackcloth, so they made no noise as they passed like ghosts along the brick street. Papa walked slightly ahead leading Richard, and Miles followed leading Robin.

As they reached the end of Quince Alley and rounded the corner, Patience turned to look back at their house, but Mama smiled at her and shook her head. "Remember Lot's wife!" she whispered.

They came to Charlie Silas's house on the next street and Patience gasped with pleasure. Painted all across the red brick front sprawled the words KING GEORGE FOREVER. She looked down at Miles, who seemed occupied with the horse. But he was grinning. She saw Papa look at the unevenly painted letters too. He glanced back at Miles, who tried to look innocent. Papa didn't say anything to Miles but swore softly to himself.

And so the Averys rode on through the sleeping streets of Philadelphia—past the church and the Assembly Hall and the Market and past Miss Edith Wormley's school where Honor had once been the star pupil and Patience had been wrapped on the head with a thimble for daydreaming.

Once they had left the city the Averys rode past the orchards and great country mansions of Pennsylvania. When they came to a grove of chestnut trees, Papa called a halt. He dismounted from Robin and vanished into the trees, to return a little while later with a powderhorn, a pouch, and a handsome Pennsylvania rifle. "I decided that these would look strange in the hands of an old farmer, so I hid them here yesterday."

"I'm glad I won't have to do all the hunting," said Miles.

"Between us, Miles, we'll keep the larder full. Now on to Albany to complete the family."

3

Papa's Adventures

Miles became aware of the hot sun first, then of noisy birds and the heavy scent of lilacs. He opened his eyes, stretched, groaned, and looked around to see where he was. Mama and Patience were still sleeping. Their faces were smudged with dirt, their skirts wrinkled and muddy from the long night's ride. Miles saw Papa up near a ridge watching the road. He remembered riding along it early that morning, four hours after they had left Philadelphia. It had been overgrown with grass and was slippery with early-morning dew. Enormous trees green-bearded with moss crowded close as the road wound its way like a stream through the woods. Mama had begged to stop and Papa had unsaddled the weary horses and made camp in a thicket of tangled lilacs.

Papa returned from the ridge. "Put your knife to work, lad!" He held up a hare in front of Miles. "Cut two forked branches and a straight one while I start the fire. As soon as this beast is roasted we'll eat."

"And you'll tell us of your adventures," said Miles.

"Why not? We have plenty of time for tales. While we are near Philadelphia we must travel by night and rest by day."

When Patience awoke half an hour later she saw Miles sitting cross-legged beside the fire turning a roasted hare slowly on a spit. The smell was delicious. "Wake up, Mama," she said. "Look at Miles. He's turned cook."

"It would be better if he turned the hare," said Mama sleepily.

"Look what I've found," said Papa, holding two broad leaves piled with strawberries.

"This is more fun than I expected," said Patience. "I thought I'd be attacked by wild animals. Instead I sleep all day and wake up to eat strawberries. Is this the way it is in the army?"

Papa laughed and poked the hare with his knife. "Not often. This is more like my days with the Indians on the Mississippi."

"Indians!"

"Oh hush, Patience," said Miles. "The Indians around here wouldn't hurt us."

"What about the massacre at—"

"Why were you living with Indians?" Mama asked. "What were you doing on the Mississippi?"

"One question at a time," said Papa. "Did you receive any letters from me after we left New York for the south?"

"The last letter came in the autumn of 1780. It told of Pensacola in the spring," said Mama. "Patience liked the description of the flowers, but Miles complained of the lack of battles."

"Why were the Loyalists sent to the South, Papa?" asked Miles. "If you'd been in the North we'd have won the war."

"It's a flattering thought, Miles, but I doubt we'd have

made much difference. When we were shipped to West Florida we were not given any reasons, but there was talk among the men that we'd been sent far away from our homes so that desertion would be less of a temptation. I heard later that there was a grand plan to sail up the Mississippi. We were to join forces with the British troops from Detroit and attack from the west through the Ohio Valley. It sounded like a wild scheme and came to naught."

"What *did* you do?" asked Miles.

"We held Pensacola and the other towns in the Floridas until gradually the Spanish recaptured every place but Pensacola. In the spring of '81 de Galvez sailed into the bay and we prepared to defend the fort. The Spaniards outnumbered us greatly, but to our surprise they did not attack. We wondered why, until a second force appeared from Mobile. By then they had ten times our number, but we had the fort. Serious fighting began and casualties were high, but we were holding our own. Then one of the powder magazines blew up. The Spaniards rushed in and our general surrendered to stop the annihilation of our troops. We lost many men. I was wounded in both legs. We learned that the enemy fire had been directed by a Loyalist deserter."

"A traitor!" said Miles. "I'd have shot the villain!"

"We had an opportunity once," said Papa. "He'd been caught attempting to desert. He was given five hundred lashes and drummed out of camp with his hands bound behind his back and a sign around his neck. They marched him towards enemy lines and left him to be finished off by the Indians or the Spaniards. But he survived and had his revenge."

"How severely wounded were you?" asked Mama. "Who looked after you?"

"The Spaniards," said Papa. "We were treated fairly

well as prisoners. De Galvez arranged to have us shipped off to New York as soon as we recovered from our wounds, and granted us parole on the condition that we would not fight Spain again.

"Two days before my ship arrived in October, smallpox broke out in the camp. I was stricken. I was left behind in quarantine with ten others."

"But you have no scars!" Mama exclaimed.

"I was fortunate. We would all have died but for an old Spanish priest who took pity on us and brought food and water each day. In the end only two of us survived. I was strong enough to help him bury the dead. I stayed with the priest—his name was de Silva—all winter. In the spring of '82 I took passage for Havana, hoping that from there I'd be able to get a ship for New York. After two days out we ran into a storm that finally wrecked the ship just east of New Orleans."

"A shipwreck!" said three voices.

With maddening slowness Papa filled his pipe with tobacco and lit it with a twig from the fire. "Don't let the hare burn," he said.

"Papa, the shipwreck!" Patience exclaimed.

"Well, the first day out there was hardly a breeze and we dawdled along like a child going to school. But on the morning of the second day a fine wind blew up and the captain ordered full sails. We made good speed all day. Just before nightfall the wind turned nasty and a storm blew up. The captain sent every man jack of the crew to reef the sails. But it was too late; the wind plucked the sailors off like apples from a tree and flung them into the sea. I was thrown against the ship's rail where I held on for dear life. I heard a tremendous crash and felt the ship shudder and leap. Lightning flashed and I could see that the main mast had snapped off. I hung on until a mountainous wave washed over the deck and then I was overboard. I felt a shock of pain and my left arm went numb—the waves had flung me against a piece of the mast. I struggled onto it and crawled under a tangle of ropes. I remember nothing after that until I awoke to find the water gently washing over me. The storm had died down and I saw that I was floating towards land.

"I freed myself and dropped into the water. My feet touched bottom and I staggered ashore and collapsed.

"I was awakened by the angry heat of the sun. I found I was on the edge of a deserted coast with nothing in sight but reedy shores. My raft had disappeared. For hours I sat there hungry and exhausted, without strength to find a way out of my hopeless situation. All I could do was pray and my prayers were answered. I saw a speck bobbing up and down on the waves. I shouted and waved my good arm and thanks be to God the speck came closer. It was one of the ship's boats rowed by two members of the crew and a Spanish merchant. They rescued me. Further along the coast we found two more survivors. Although we searched as well as we could along those misbegotten shores, we found no one else. And so we rowed to New Orleans."

Here Papa stopped and smiled to see far-away expressions on his listeners' faces. "How is the hare, Miles?"

With a start Miles returned from Louisiana. He took the hare off the spit and carefully tore it into pieces and handed them around.

"What happened then?" he asked, licking his fingers.

"Then I spent three months in jail."

"James! What had you done?" Mama set the roast meat down and looked at him indignantly. Her father's tales of war had always been of heroic acts in battle, daring and brave.

Miles was also puzzled. A battle won by a traitor...left behind by the army...shipwrecked and jailed—Grandpa Dawe's campaigns had never been like this.

Papa noticed their growing consternation. He smiled at Patience.

"My exploits seem to displease your mother and brother."

"They like war stories," she said. "I don't. They give me nightmares. I like yours better. Tell about New Orleans."

"It's crowded with smugglers and pirates—sinners of every description, all chattering in French and Spanish. They did little but fan themselves and sleep through the scorching afternoons and drink and fight in low dens all night."

"But prison, James!"

"Don't take on, Abigail. I was in a tavern trying to arrange passage to the West Indies when a brawl started and because I was there, I was thrown in jail along with a gang of pirates and fur-trappers."

"How horrible!"

"The pirates were the vilest bunch I ever met, but the trappers were excellent men. Several of them had spent years with the Indians and knew their languages and customs well. It was a most interesting three months. Uncomfortable, though."

"How did you get out?" asked Miles.

"New Orleans is a dry patch in a swamp and the water seeps in everywhere. We were all in one large cell together— pirates, trappers, thieves, and cutthroats. The jail was partly underground and more like a dungeon. There was a pool of slime at one end and when it rained the water rose. The guards would throw us buckets and we worked as a brigade, passing the buckets from man to man up the steps, through the cell door and along the corridor out of the jail. We were heavily guarded when we worked the buckets and if anyone tried to escape he was shot.

"Early in September it rained for three days, and we thought we'd drown for our sins. They threw the buckets in at last and we bailed until nightfall on the third day. The relief platoon was late and our guards were tired. They tried to force us to go back into the dungeon for the night but we decided we might as well be shot as drowned, so we attacked them and most of us escaped. I joined the trappers and we borrowed a boat and set off up the Mississippi. To make a long story short I reached Oswego and came down the route we are now taking north."

Papa tapped out his pipe. "That's enough from me. I'd like to hear more about how you managed in Philadelphia." He put his pipe away. "Oh, I forgot. I lost the rest of my papers in the shipwreck, but I meant to show Miles my parole from the Spanish government."

He produced a small much-worn packet from his pouch and handed it to Miles. Miles opened it and unfolded a sheet of paper with a scarlet seal at the bottom. Patience leaned over to see.

"What does it say?" asked Miles. "I can't understand the words. Is it in Spanish?"

"Yes," said Papa. "I couldn't read it either when I got it, but one benefit of being wounded and left in Pensacola for so long was that I learned some Spanish. It just says that I am free to leave Pensacola and that I give my word as an officer not to bear arms against Spain and her possessions."

He licked his fingers and rubbed them on his clothes, then looked guiltily at Mama. "Forgive me, Abby. I must relearn my town manners."

4

The Lonesome Unicorn

A large raindrop fell on Patience's nose.

"Miles, stop it!" she said, turning over on the moss and sitting up. But Miles was still asleep under a nearby tree beside the horses. Mama and Papa were sleeping beside Patience under a small shelter of cedar branches. Patience moved further under to protect herself from the rain. Then she lay back and began to think about the long weeks since they had left Philadelphia.

At first they had travelled by night, slowly and painfully. Then they began to travel cautiously by day. This was faster but more dangerous. They had trotted across low stone bridges over treacherous crossings. They had picnicked in flower-strewn meadows and hidden in swamps for hours at a time, hungry and cold, as troops of militia passed along the road. But even worse than the threat of capture, or the danger of attack by bears or wolves, were the mosquitoes that swarmed about them in clouds whenever they stopped to rest. All four Averys were red and swollen from their bites. The only remedy was to make a fire and stand in the smoke, but this made their eyes sting and was just another form of torture.

Patience watched the rain dance in the pools that were forming in the clearing. She mumbled to herself: "At least it keeps the mosquitoes away."

"Now you are starting to look on the bright side," said Papa with his eyes still closed.

Mama stretched, opened her eyes, and groaned when she saw the rain.

"Another night spent outside in this weather will kill us all, James," said Mama. "Surely we can risk a night in an inn?"

"I'd like to reach the Hudson first. Perhaps the rain will stop soon."

But the rain drizzled on all through the morning and the road turned to mud under the horses' hooves. The way ahead grew steadily darker and more threatening. As the hot afternoon wore on, thunder began to growl between the hills like angry bears spoiling for a fight. The weather wore their feelings raw.

"Are we near Albany yet?" asked Patience.

"For the tenth time, no!" Papa snapped. "And if you ask me once more, I'll leave you to walk to Canada by yourself!"

Miles smiled unkindly at Patience. *"Patientia spurca est."*

"Use your Latin while you can. There won't be an academy for you to go to in Cataraqui, Miles Avery. You'll have to be a farmer."

"Thick-skull," said Miles. "I shall be a cavalry officer in the British army. They fight *real* battles."

"You young popinjay!" said Papa. "You already have

enough arrogance to be a British officer, but until they send you your commission I'll thank you to act like a gentleman. It is excessively rude to insult your sister in a language she cannot understand."

"Very well. Patience is a nasty girl," said Miles.

"I am not!" shrilled Patience.

"*Miles!*" thundered Papa.

"Hush, hush!" implored Mama. "We are all tired and wet and miserable. Surely, James, we can stop at an inn."

"It is dangerous."

"Stumbling through this swampy country in the dark and the damp is also dangerous," Mama argued. "We will get wet to the skin and take fevers and an ague, and I did not bring enough Venice Treacle to dose us all."

"Perhaps you are right," said Papa.

The storm broke furiously even as he spoke. They rode on for half an hour in drenching rain.

"There's something up ahead," Miles called. He halted Richard and waited. Papa, with Patience huddled under his coat, drew level with Miles and Mama. The rain guttered off the wide brim of Papa's black hat. "It's an inn and we'll stop there."

"Perhaps we should journey on after all," said Mama looking around doubtfully as they rode up to a creaking sign. The huge dark shape of the inn lurked behind a row of tall sycamores that swayed and groaned in the wind. Its sagging shutters banged an eerie chorus to the moaning of the trees.

"The Lonesome Unicorn," Miles said as they passed the sign and turned into the courtyard.

"I don't like the look of it," said Mama. "What if it is swarming with rebels?"

"Poppycock!" said Papa. He tied the horses to the hitching post and helped Mama and Patience to dismount. "Take the bags in, Miles. If we don't change into dry clothes, even Mama's Venice Treacle won't save us from chills and fevers.''

Papa shouldered a bag and walked up to the door. He lifted the doorknocker—a brass unicorn with an evil expression—and banged it hard.

"Perhaps—" began Mama just as the door opened. Before them stood a short fat man with black hair combed in flat curls across his brow.

"Grafton Fevergrure, my honeys," the man said. "Formerly a peruke-maker at the sign of the Black Wigg in Boston, now host at the Lonesome Unicorn. Please enter."

The door banged behind them and the Averys gathered in a dark hall. In the sudden quiet Miles could hear the water dripping from his clothes.

"Welcome to the Lonesome Unicorn. We have been as dull as beetles here since this dreadful war."

Down the long shadowed hall a tall figure was approaching with dainty steps.

"Tilly, my dear—this is my daughter, Tilly Minching."

Patience wondered how a round little man who looked like a firkin of butter could have a daughter who looked like a rake. "Silly Tilly," she whispered to Miles.

Tilly was wearing a gown that was strangely elaborate for such a remote spot. Her powdered hair was piled high upon her head and she glittered with jewellery. In her arms she held a cat.

"Such a horrid night...the dear children," Tilly twittered. She swept Mama and Papa a deep curtsey.

"D'you have a room that's cheap and dry?" Papa asked.

"Indeed, indeed," said Fevergrure. "The whole of our humble inn is yours."

"Where are you bound?" Tilly chirped.

"Albany," said Papa.

"Ah yes," said Grafton Fevergrure. "The Albanians are splendid fellows, splendid—but beware, they do love to bamboozle strangers, and they are as sharp as a snipe at a snout, are they not, Tilly? My grandmother hailed from Albany," he added. "But come, you are up to your middles in mud. We must provide some beds and a small collation for all. Two rooms for the price of one tonight. We are not overcrowded."

"Miles and I will tend to the horses," said Papa.

Fevergrure led Mama and Patience down the hall, up stairs, around corners, up more stairs, and around more corners. Patience held Mama's hand tightly; the candlelight flickered and cats' eyes flashed out of the darkness from windows, doorways, and corridors. Cats seemed to be crouching everywhere.

At last they came to their rooms, which were large and surprisingly cheerful.

"This will suit us well," said Mama.

The innkeeper beamed affably. "You will be ready for supper and we will have roast beef, gooseberry fool, and a chunk of cheese," he said. "Afterwards we may have a little music and further conversation about Albany. Does little miss remember her dancing lessons? Perhaps she will do me the favour of hopping a dance. I was a dancing-master before I made perukes. Rigadoons and paspies, Spanish fandangoes and Devonshire jigs, then contra-dances—the Innocent Maid, Blue Bonnets, the Orange Tree—I knew them all." He gave a sigh while his feet cut a caper, almost by themselves.

"Oh yes!" Patience cried eagerly, but Mama frowned.

"Splendid!" said Grafton Fevergrure, and he left the room.

"What bliss to sleep in a bed again," said Mama. She

tested the mattress. "Hardly a bed of down, but better than a pile of wet branches. Change into your dry things, poppet, while I hang up these soggy rags."

She pulled rumpled clothes from the bag and began to drape the wet ones over a straight-backed chair and a wash-stand. "They'll take all night to dry this way, but it's too hot for a fire. How I loathe these sticky stormy nights!"

"I don't trust that man," Mama said when Papa and Miles came in.

"Nor I," said Papa in a muffled voice as he stripped off his wet clothes. "They're a queer lot of people."

"What ragamuffins we are," sighed Mama when she hung the last of the clothes up to dry. "Who would have thought we would come to this?"

An hour later they were working their way back through the maze that led to the front of the inn. "Guard your tongues, now!" Papa warned as they neared the sound of voices.

"I feel all over like a jelly," said Patience, but her fears subsided with the heartening smell of roast beef. The excellent dinner improved their spirits and they enjoyed Fever-grure's stories of Boston.

At the end of the meal their host triumphantly carried in a silver bowl. "Cold raspberry shrub!" he announced. "Grafton Fevergrure's shrub was as famous as his perukes in Boston. Will the young master and the little miss have a cup?"

"No, indeed!" said Mama.

"Music, we must have music!" the innkeeper called. "Tilly, my dear, would you oblige?"

In a high, surprisingly sweet voice, Tilly sang of Polly Wand and her sad fate:

Come all you bold huntsmen who follow the gun,
Beware of a shooting by the setting of the sun,
For her true love went hunting and shot in the dark,
And woe! and alas! Polly Wand was his mark.

"A fine song," said Papa, applauding. "Now to bed. We have far to go tomorrow."

"But first a toast," said Fevergrure, his eyes shining like black beetles in the candlelight. He held his cup high. "Drink damnation to King George and all the rascals about him!"

Without hesitation Papa said "Amen" and finished his drink. Miles bolted from the room.

"Your young lad seems distressed," said Fevergrure, pulling his forelock.

"Too much good food," said Papa, rising. "Goodnight."

They retraced their way to their rooms.

"These antics of Miles' may cost us dearly," Papa said.

"But I wondered at you too," said Mama. "How could you drink that villainous rebel toast? It would have choked me."

"A toast never choked anyone, but a gang of 'patriots' might," said Papa. "That innkeeper is suspicious enough already. Where is Miles?"

"Leave him, James, I beg of you," said Mama. "We're all so tired."

"I like his high spirits, but Miles must learn to curb his temper," said Papa.

"What a poking pair those Fevergrures are," growled Miles when Patience came into their room. "I'd like to clout them both—the old fright and that smirking fellow. I'm sure he's up to no good."

"Oh Miles, I shan't sleep a wink!"

Miles opened the door that led out to the balcony. Cool night air flowed into the room; the storm was passing. Miles stepped out onto the balcony. He leaned on the railing and watched the tree tops sway. The storm was to the west now and occasional flashes of lightning appeared like cracks in the black sky. A pale moon in the east made the wet stable roof glisten.

Patience followed Miles and leaned over to try to pick the rain-drenched honeysuckle that twined its way up from the yard.

"I'll get a piece for you," said Miles. As he reached over the railing he saw a light at the far end of the courtyard. Voices carried by the wind floated up from the shadows. He pulled Patience back into the room.

"Someone's below," he said. "I'm going down to see who it is."

Miles went out on the balcony again to a post wreathed in vines. He slid over the railing and down the post to the courtyard.

Tilly Minching, swathed in a long black cloak, shielded a lantern for a squat figure that stood beside a horse at the far end of the courtyard. Miles crept towards them, keeping close to the wall under the balcony. He saw Fevergrure swing into the saddle.

"I am going for Obadiah," the innkeeper said. "His feeble brain and strong arms are all we need to deal with these Tories." He rode out into the darkness. Tilly stared after him, then slowly returned to the inn.

Miles ran back and gave a low whistle underneath Patience's window. She appeared immediately at the balcony railing.

"Tell Papa we must leave at once! Fevergrure knows we're Tories. I'll saddle the horses."

Patience rushed inside. "Papa!" she called in a low voice as she struggled to open the door between the two rooms. "Papa, come quickly!"

The door opened and Papa appeared, buckling his belt. He listened in silence to her story.

"I feared as much," he said.

Mama was already tying their wet clothes into a bundle. "Drop this over the balcony with Miles' bag," she said. "We can carry the rest."

They made their way quickly towards the front hall. Mama and Patience kept close to Papa. They came to the room where they had eaten and Papa motioned to them to be quiet. They could see Tilly moving about, talking to herself.

"Grafton will punish 'em. He'll tar and feather 'em. He'll throw them in the pond to cool their loyalty. He'll—" Waving a tankard in the air, she began to sing "God save great Washington. God damn King George—" The song ended in a screech as she caught sight of Patience tiptoeing past the door.

"Grafton will catch you and teach the young master to drink a proper toast!" she cried, rushing out after them.

Tilly was still screaming abuse at them from the door of the inn as they mounted the horses.

"Destruction take your rebel inn!" shouted Mama defiantly, with a wave of her arm.

A bolt of lightning flashed across the sky and struck one of the sycamores. The giant tree groaned and with a loud grinding sigh toppled slowly across the roof of the inn.

"Witch! Witch!" Tilly shrieked.

5

Arrival in Albany

Miles and Papa reined the horses at the crumbling edge of a cliff. It was early dawn. Below in the valley lay the black hulk of a barn. Behind them stretched ten miles of a washed-out trail, made almost impassable by mud and rock slides.

"Can we sleep there?" asked Miles. "It looks deserted. The farmhouse must have burned down ages ago."

"Go down ahead of us, Miles, and wave if all is well," said Papa.

Miles climbed quickly and carefully down the cliff, ran across the field and into the shadows of the barn.

"He seems so small down there," said Mama. "I hope it isn't another rebel den."

The minutes passed slowly and Patience counted under her breath, "210, 211, 212 . . . There he is and he's waving!"

They followed a path down the cliff and made their way across a muddy field to the barn.

"It's snug and dry," Miles reported as he led them inside. He made straw beds while Papa rubbed down the exhausted horses. "Should we keep a watch for Fevergrure?" Miles asked as they finished.

"There were three forks in that trail," said Papa, "and thanks to the rain we left no tracks, so I don't think we need worry about our stout friend."

They slept soundly and wakened to a clear sunny afternoon and the cheerful chirping of birds in the rafters. Swallows swept in and out through gaps in the walls.

After Patience found the remains of a vegetable garden and an overgrown raspberry patch, they decided to stay another day. Mama's worries about Fevergrure were offset by her pleasure at finding the vegetables.

During the rest of their trip to Albany they avoided inns. Luckily the rain stayed away and the nights were cool and pleasant under the stars. Papa led them by Indian trails across hills and through forests until they reached the Hudson River.

"How far are we from Albany now?" asked Miles as they travelled north along the river road.

"I was hoping that Patience would ask," said Papa. "She has asked at least twice a day since we left and at last I can say we are almost there. In less than an hour, Patience, you will see Honor again and meet your cousins."

"Nicholas has two snakes and Philip has a dog and three rabbits," Miles said.

"Meg has a kitten and Caroline has a ground squirrel," added Patience. "And Caroline has black hair and is freckled as a mushroom, like me," laughed Miles.

"Honor wrote that they even had a porcupine," Mama told Papa, "but it ate the verandah and Stephen insisted that it go back to the woods."

The late afternoon sun cast a glow across the road before

them and dappled the well-kept gardens and orchards beside it with a green-golden light. The Averys looked curiously at the hillocks of Indian corn, with potatoes, gourds, and cucumbers growing in rows between them. These large country gardens were different from the neat box-edged gardens of Philadelphia.

On the other side of the road wild grape vines, heavy with fruit, spilled temptingly down the river-bank, but Miles and Patience had already discovered that they were not yet sweet enough to eat.

Then they saw Albany sprawled before them on a slope by the river. Mountains loomed blue in the west, and on a steep hill in the middle of the town sat a great stone fort.

As they rode into the city they heard the church bells chime six o'clock. The solemn melody mingled pleasantly with the cheerful jingle of cowbells as the cows returned from pasture, each to its owner's stable.

The streets were merry with children playing, while their elders gossiped and rocked on the porch that stood in front of each house. Noisy shouts of cries of "You're out!" cut across the grave conversations of stoutly prosperous merchants promenading under the trees.

Robin and Richard, sensing the end of the day's journey, picked up their pace.

"Which is Aunt Sally's cow, do you suppose?" said Patience. "Can we have our supper on the steps like the Albanian children?"

"I hope we get some milk," Miles said, looking critically at the way some boys were handling a ball.

"Contain yourselves, gluttons," said Papa. "We are nearly there. The Vanderpflugs live just on the other side of town."

They rode along the hilly streets, past tall gabled houses with Dutch-tiled roofs and scrubbed diamond windows that twinkled in the late afternoon sun. The low eaves of the houses hung halfway into the streets.

"Here is the orchard!" said Papa. "We are almost there."

But something was wrong. The trees were stripped of their fruit, and in many places the fence was broken. Its sagging posts looked like grey crooked dwarfs. The Averys rode on in an uneasy silence and came at last to the house.

It was just as Mama had described it, with heavy shutters and a weather vane shaped like a lion. But there was no welcoming light in the window, no frolicking swarm of cousins and animals. The great front door creaked mournfully as Papa pushed it open.

Before them was a large room with an open timbered ceiling. The last rays of the sun shone through the cobwebs that covered the shattered windows and fell upon hacked chairs, broken china, and scattered books.

Mama sank down upon what was left of a chair and covered her face with her hands. Papa, his face tight with anger, muttered: "The scoundrels! This is monstrous!"

"What happened?" Patience asked Miles, who stood silently beside her. "Why is everything helter-skelter? Where is Honor?"

"The mob," said Miles, picking up a torn book. "The villains have gone on a rampage and sacked the house."

"I shall go distracted," Mama moaned. "What shall we do?"

"You'll be the Vanderpflugs' relations from Philadelphia."

They turned and saw a hollow-cheeked woman smoothing her apron with reddened hands.

"Where is my sister?" Mama asked her plaintively.

"Gone," the woman said.

"Not dead?" Mama asked quietly.

"No." The woman hesitated, and her thin face softened as she looked at the bewildered family standing in the middle of the desolate room.

"You'll be the young sister," she said to Patience. "Honor used to tell my Pieter stories about you before he died of a flux."

"Who are you?" Papa asked.

"Widow Cuyler. A neighbour."

"Madam," he said, "what has happened to our family?"

"They took a sloop to New York just before the mob attacked the house," she answered.

Mama burst into tears. "Poor Honor!" she sobbed. "We must follow her to New York."

"Try to be calm," said Papa. "They escaped, and for that we must be thankful. Rest assured that Stephen will take care of Honor." He began to light his pipe, and Miles saw that his hand was not quite steady. "They might have sailed for England or the West Indies or Canada, and we have no means of tracing them just now. Our only hope is to reach Canada before winter comes. Once we are settled on our land, I shall write to the Governor in Quebec and the authorities in England and they will surely help us to find them."

"I will bring you supper here as soon as it is dark," said Mrs Cuyler gently. "But you must leave Albany early in the morning before the neighbours are about. As you can see, they have no fondness for Tories."

"What shall we do if the rebels come again and find us here?" Patience said to Miles an hour later as they sat in the dusk eating bread and cheese amidst the wreckage in Aunt Sally's pretty room.

"May they roast in hell!" said Miles fiercely. "Just let one come near me and I'll send him there!"

6

Alf Brown

Miles awoke at sunrise. Mama and Patience were huddled asleep on the floor in the midst of the broken furniture. Papa, guarding the door, stared blankly at the desolation of the room. He motioned to Miles to follow him into the garden.

"Get the horses ready and be as quiet as possible. We must leave before Albany begins to stir, but I want your mother to sleep while she can. 'Twill help her to face the prospect of continuing the journey without Honor."

Only now, walking through the dew-wet grass to the horses, did Miles realize how much he had been looking forward to seeing Honor again and to meeting his unknown relatives. All of them—sister, cousins, uncle, and aunt, even the animals—would have been reinforcement in their travels through this alien land.

A broken shutter banged and he looked back at the ruined house. The lion weather vane, still standing erect on the tiled roof, faced north.

"Perhaps it's a sign. I'll tell Patience. It will cheer her up."

When he returned to the house after saddling the horses he found Patience and Mama investigating the contents of smashed drawers and broken wardrobes.

"What are you doing?"

"Hunting to see what the mob overlooked," said Mama with a wavery smile. "Perhaps I can salvage something of Sally's."

"Look at this!" said Patience, her voice muffled in the depths of a heavy chest. She held up a sheet of paper.

"Honor must have been sketching again instead of tending to her sewing," said Mama. She looked at the picture. It was a lighthearted drawing of Aunt Sally's family with everyone clutching an animal. Even Aunt Sally held a supercilious cat, while Uncle Stephen seemed to be balancing a very large and indignant crow on one shoulder.

"I wish someone had sketched Honor," she said wistfully. "We have no likeness of her at all."

"Someone did!" cried Patience, who had gone on rummaging in the chest. She pulled out another smaller drawing. It was crude, but it was undoubtedly Honor.

Mama took it from her eagerly and studied it for a long minute. "Sally must have done it," she said quietly. She fumbled in her bag until she found the locket Papa had given her before he went to war. Folding the picture carefully, she fitted it inside.

"Now, my dears," she said, her eyes glistening with unshed tears, "let's see what we have left for breakfast."

There was little reason for lingering in the desolate house. After hastily eating the remains of Mrs Cuyler's food, they rode out of Albany.

No one felt like talking. They rode slowly and silently, like the remains of a small defeated army, unaware of the passing scene. The road followed the river. On the left, fields of wheat and flax rippled in the light morning breeze. Clumps of water-beeches and poplars shaded them on the river side. It was already hot.

Finally Papa roused himself.

"This won't do," he said. "We can't mope all the way to Canada. We face enough difficulties without that."

"I feel as if we're riding further away from Honor and Sally all the time," said Mama in a low voice.

"If they've fled to Canada," said Papa, "we may be coming closer to them."

Mama sniffled, nodded, and rubbed her eyes. As they rode on, she began to talk of the past when she and Aunt Sally had attended assemblies, ox-roasts, and parades in the garrison towns where their father had been stationed.

The hills along the river were smothered with wild grape vines; some of them had even climbed over the trees and covered them, making them bend like aged pedlars beneath their weight.

The Averys turned away from the Hudson and began to follow the Mohawk towards the mountains.

The trail grew more difficult. They walked in single file, leading the horses, and had to rest more often as the afternoon wore on. They came to a bend in the trail at the top of a small hill and Papa decided to make camp for the night. Miles went down to the river to fish while Patience gathered grapes and berries and Papa collected wood for the fire.

Mama cleared an area for sleeping, all the while thinking of Honor and trying to imagine her safe in England or Canada. She was interrupted by a shout from the river and looked down to see Miles waving and holding up a big fish.

After supper Patience and Mama sat on a big rock talking about Honor and watching the sunset. Papa and Miles sat by the fire cleaning their guns.

"Don't say anything to worry your mother," Papa said, "but we are moving into bear country now. Your fowling-piece won't stop an angry bear but keep it handy anyway."

It grew dark and Papa piled up the fire as they settled down for the night.

Dum-Dum De-Dum-Dum.

"What's that?" said Patience.

The steady beat, sounding back along the trail, became louder.

"Hide behind that rock away from the fire," Papa said. "It sounds like the drum of an army patrol." He picked up his rifle and moved off into the shadows.

Miles took his gun and joined Mama and Patience behind the rock.

Dum-Dum De-Dum-Dum.

It was almost upon them.

Dum-Dum De-Dum-Dum.

There was a final brisk roll, and into the firelight marched a ragged boy with an army drum and a pair of boots slung over his shoulder.

He set his drum down carefully and looked around in surprise.

"No one 'ome?" he asked loudly.

The Averys emerged carrying their guns.

"Stone a crow but you're an unfriendly bunch!" the boy exclaimed.

Papa laughed and put down his rifle.

"What do you mean by parading through the woods in

the dark scaring us half to death?" asked Miles angrily. "Who are you?"

The drummer boy ignored him and turned to Papa. "Alf Brown reporting, General. Late of His Majesty's army and on me way to Canada."

He looked a little older than Miles, with blue eyes, an upturned nose, and hair so fair that it seemed almost white. In place of a uniform, he wore—it was hard to tell what he wore. Shirts of at least three different colours showed through the ragged holes of the one he wore on top, and he seemed to be wearing breeches inside his breeches to cover the holes in the knees and seat. Around his neck was knotted a red handkerchief.

"Me old Auntie Cuyler told me you folks were going to Canada. Can I go with you? I brought me own grub." Alf unpacked a sausage and a loaf of bread and handed them to Mama. Then he reached back into his bag and produced two pork pies that he handed to Patience. From the bottom of the bag he took a small jug of whisky and handed it to Papa. Then he turned to Miles with a smile. "Sorry, mate, that's all I got."

"Did Mrs Cuyler give you all this?" asked Mama.

"Well, not exactly. She gave me the bread and the rest I picked up from the good citizens of Albany," said Alf.

"I suppose you stole them," said Mama, looking sadly at the pork pies.

"Oh, no, Milady. More like collectin' an old debt, it was."

"But you're English," said Patience. "How can Mrs Cuyler be your aunt?"

Still smiling angelically, Alf said: "It's a long story. I was borned in London, that's all I know. Growed up in the poor's house and a horrid life that was. I ran away from there and lived merry as a tadpole, till one day I was sent to prison just for borrowing a flitch of bacon from a butcher. Well, I couldn't stand that, so off to the army I went, soon's I escaped, to be a drummer boy. Been at every battle, I 'ave— Saratoga, Yorktown, Bunker Hill.''

"How old are you?'' asked Papa, while Miles and Patience stared at Alf admiringly.

"Twelve or thirteen or thereabouts.''

"Bunker Hill was nine years ago. An infant drummer boy is indeed a rarity,'' said Papa. "How did you land in Albany?''

"Well, your Lordship...'' Alf twirled his drumsticks restlessly and gave Papa a look of melting honesty. "Your Grace, I—''

"Stop the toad-eating, boy, and tell the truth!''

"When the troops came back, there I was in Albany.''

"British troops are an uncommon sight in Albany these days. Were you by any chance with the Continental Army?''

Admiration shone on Alf's face. "What a one you are to ferret out the truth, Gen—''

"A turncoat!'' Miles looked at him in outrage.

"Oh no, young master, but a poor orphan has to live as best he can, so I follow me drum wherever it takes me. And the borrowin's good in an army.'' He beamed at them all. "One army's like another, as long as I can play me drum and pick up a few baubles here and there.''

"Then Mrs Cuyler isn't your real aunt,'' said Miles angrily.

"Well, she missed her Pieter.''

This time Papa was not amused. "You mean you imposed on the grief of that poor woman?''

"Now, sir, it helped me and it made her happy to 'ave someone young to fuss over."

"I should send you back," began Papa.

"Oh, please, sir—please take me to Canada. Give me a chance, sir. I'll stick to the straight and narrow."

"I doubt that you have ever been on that path," was Papa's comment. "But who are we to turn away a homeless waif?" And so Alf stayed.

Papa and Miles and Alf laboured for two days to clear the trail of several huge trees that blocked it completely for half a mile ahead.

They all reacted differently to Alf. Mama fussed over him. She could not believe that an honest heart did not lurk beneath such an angelic though grubby exterior. Besides, he was willing to help and was skilled at finding the roots and berries that made up a large part of their scanty meals.

Miles tried unsuccessfully to ignore him. The only thing that seemed worse to him than a rebel was a turncoat. But he was fascinated by Alf just the same.

To Patience he brought dismay and delight. For no reason that she could understand, he would jab her in the ribs, but ten minutes later he would make her a willow whistle or bring her a bird's nest from the fallen trees that lay across the river like leafy bridges.

Inspired by the ease with which Alf scampered across the massive fallen trunks, Patience ventured out herself one day and settled down to read in a green-leaved bower over the river.

"This is fun!" She smiled at Alf as he cartwheeled along the trunk to join her. She closed her book and fanned herself with a spray of leaves.

"It's near the first time I've seen you smile," he remarked, swinging his feet perilously close to the torrent that foamed beneath. "You're not a very cheerful lot, you and your family. I've seen merrier faces in a hangman's noose."

"It's my sister Honor," said Patience. "We may never see her again."

"You misses her?" Alf looked surprised.

"Of course. Wouldn't you?"

"I've never had nobody to miss," he said. "But there's still four of you. That seems more than enough family for anyone."

"It's not the same," said Patience. "What if we never find her?"

Alf pulled up his feet and sat cross-legged on the tree trunk. "I'm good at finding things," he said.

Alf had even fewer possessions than the Averys. Mama insisted on washing his four shirts and three pairs of breeches, much to his disgust. "Be careful or they'll fall apart," he said as he unwillingly took them off and wrapped himself in a blanket.

Alf's greatest treasure, apart from his drum, which he allowed no one to touch, was a pair of magnificent boots. He polished them every day, and before putting them on he always scrubbed his feet.

"Where did you get those boots?" asked Patience, watching one day as he scraped at the stubborn patches of dirt that clung to them.

"They're me old uncle's boots. Left them to me in his will, he did."

"I thought you were a foundling," said Miles.

Alf paused in his polishing. "I've never met such truth-mongers in all me born days,'' he said. ''I recollect now that I found 'em on a battlefield.''

''Where?''

''Lying there, more or less.''

The horrid truth dawned. ''You stole them from a corpse!''

Alf pulled a boot onto an immaculate foot. ''Now wouldn't it be wicked to let a fine pair of boots like this moulder away by themselves in the rain and mud?'' he said. ''Think on it.'' Whistling, he shuffled off.

One day Patience asked Alf: ''Don't you ever wonder about your parents? Perhaps you're the son of a noble lord or an earl.''

''An orange girl and an actor more like.''

''Wasn't there anything to show who you were—a family seal or a ring?''

Alf seemed undisturbed by his lack of family. ''Bare as a plucked chicken I was,'' he said, admiring his boots.

7

Oswego

The signs of the north country grew more frequent as the hot days of July passed into the cool nights of August. The trail was often blocked and at times it disappeared altogether. The only other travellers they met were Indian hunting parties. Miles was impressed by the casual and friendly way Papa met these groups. The stories that were told in Philadelphia about the Indians of the Mohawk Valley were the sort to give nightmares. He knew that the Mohawk had fought for the King, but he couldn't banish the stories entirely from his mind.

Gradually the country became flatter and they left the mountains, travelling through gently rolling woodland until they reached a small river flowing north. They journeyed along its bank.

"We're making good progress now," Papa said one morning. "With luck we will have just enough time to build our log house before winter starts."

"What will happen if we are late?" Patience asked.

"I'd rather not spoil a pleasant morning thinking about that. Instead I'll give you some good news. Look ahead."

They saw the river open into a lake that stretched to the horizon. High and lonely on a bluff, overlooking both river and lake, stood a fort with the British flag flopping in the breeze. The Averys gave a loud cheer and Alf joined in enthusiastically, pleased to see them all so happy.

They followed a path from the river up to the top of the bluff and rode over a drawbridge into the fort. The sentry was a young soldier with red hair. He was even more freckled than Miles.

"We are Loyalists from Philadelphia bound for Cataraqui," said Papa.

"Go straight through and report over there." The sentry pointed across the square to a door. "The stables are around to the left. Take your horses there and they'll be looked after." He inspected Robin and Richard critically and then smiled. "They're in good shape. Some of the Loyalists who came this summer drove their poor beasts into the ground. I hate to see a horse mistreated."

As he spoke, an officer came around the corner and the sentry snapped to attention.

"Loyalists from Philadelphia, sir," he said.

The young officer bowed to Mama. "Lieutenant Trudgett at your service, Ma'am. Welcome to British soil— what's left of it here, that is. Come with me and I'll show you to your quarters."

As they walked across the square he ordered a passing soldier to take Miles and the horses to the stables.

"There's room in the barracks for a thousand men," Trudgett said, "but we have scarce twenty here at present. We keep an eye out for Americans trying to sneak through to trade in Canada, and we help occasional Loyalists like you across the lake, while maintaining this outpost. There's a batteau leaving in a few days and you can have passage on that.''

He ushered them into a large room lined with narrow wooden beds. "You can have this room to yourselves. It isn't very comfortable, but if you have travelled from Philadelphia you will have endured worse accommodation.''

"Indeed we have, and thank you,'' said Mama, sitting down gratefully on the bed.

"Come to the Captain's quarters when you are ready, sir,'' the young officer said to Papa. "Meanwhile I'll send you some provisions.'' He saluted and left.

A moment later Miles staggered in under the weight of the saddlebags.

"Where is Alf? I thought he was with you,'' said Papa.

"He was, but he went off to report. He said he'd have to explain how he was captured and imprisoned by the rebels, and how he'd escaped and fought his way back to rejoin his regiment.''

"But that's a lie,'' said Patience.

"I told him that,'' said Miles, "but he said he had to maintain the incorruptible traditions of the British soldier— even if he had to lie to do it.''

Papa laughed. "Alf's cheerful ways helped us over the black time after we left Albany. We wouldn't want to say anything that would cause him to be whipped as a deserter, would we Miles?''

"That's true,'' said Miles, sitting down on a bed with a groan of relief. "But I won't tell any lies for the rogue, and I hope I don't have any soldiers like *him* when I become an officer in the army.''

"There are more like him where Alf came from, lad, and

if you mean to follow in your grandfather's footsteps, you'll have to learn more about the army than the glory of campaigns."

They were interrupted by a soldier who brought a jug of cider, with some bread and cheese and roasted meat.

When they had finished eating, Alf appeared, wearing a new shirt over his old ones and a new pair of breeches. Both breeches and shirt were several sizes too big.

"They said I had to tidy up a bit, but they didn't give me much choice," he said, surveying himself proudly.

"Give me those clothes," said Mama. "I can cut them down for you so that at least you won't trip over yourself."

"I'm glad they didn't hang you as a deserter," said Patience.

"No fear. The army needs heroes like me what fought the rebels."

Miles stood up. "I think I'll go for a walk before our hero asks me to polish his boots."

"No offence, mate. I'll catch up with you soon as Milady cuts me breeches down to size."

They spent the next three days exploring the fort and its surroundings, while the batteau, damaged by a storm on the way over, was repaired for the trip back across the lake to Cataraqui.

Miles became friends with Thomas Trudgett, who was only nineteen himself. They went hunting wildfowl together when Thomas was off duty.

"I want to join the army when I'm old enough," Miles told him when they were on their way back to the fort after an afternoon's hunting. "My grandfather was a colonel in the Dragoons. When can I join up and what do I have to do? I'll be thirteen next birthday."

"You have the spirit for it," said Tom, "but you will need money to buy your commission, you know, and to support you. The first few years in the army are expensive. My uncle paid for my commission when I was sixteen. That was in 1781. I was sent to Canada in the spring of '82. If your father lost everything in the war then your army career will have to wait."

"We might prosper in Cataraqui," said Miles. "I have to help Papa build a house and I can't go away until we find my sister . . ."

"Patience told me about the flight of your relatives from Albany. It's a sad affair, but they did escape and probably they fared better than you did. At least they didn't have to travel overland. The main problem is to locate them."

"If they did escape and if Honor is safe," said Miles.

Thomas stopped suddenly. "Never *if*—*if* we escape, *if* we survive, *if* we win the battle. You will learn to say *when*. *When* we win the battle, never *if*." He smiled sheepishly. "I'm sorry. I'm talking to you like a new recruit." He looked at the darkening sky. "We must hurry. We sail for Cataraqui tomorrow morning and I have work to finish."

The batteau was loaded early the next morning. Mama and Papa said farewell to Captain Forbes, the commandant of the fort, and thanked him for his hospitality during their short stay.

Mama was helped aboard the batteau by Thomas Trudgett, who was in charge.

"Will it be a rough crossing?" she asked somewhat anxiously.

"No Ma'am, I don't think so. The wind is fair. And if there is a storm, we'll just toss a black dog overboard as the Indians do. We should reach the islands tonight," he told

Papa, who had followed Mama aboard, "and we'll be in Cataraqui by tomorrow afternoon."

The crew rowed the batteau slowly out into the blue waters of the lake. Trudgett ordered the sail hoisted and as it caught the breeze the big clumsy boat floated smoothly along the coast without human aid. They watched the fort grow smaller in the distance.

Miles, Alf, and Patience lay near the bow and watched the sunlight catch the spray that flashed and sparkled high in the air. Thomas called to them as he made his way astern. "Take care when you go aft. I don't want anyone overboard. You'd drown before I could turn the boat around."

"He's a good 'un," said Alf. "Reminds me of me big brother, he does."

"You're an orphan, remember?" Miles said irritably.

"So? Orphans can have brothers. Sisters too. Aunts even." Alf felt less sure about aunts so he dropped the subject.

The day passed and by evening they reached some green-forested islands as Trudgett had predicted.

The crew manoeuvred the boat into the lee of an island and drew it up on a beach beyond the grasp of the water. The soldiers heaped huge bundles of brushwood upon a fallen cedar tree and started a roaring fire. While Miles and Alf explored the island, Patience toasted her toes comfortably and watched a haunch of venison roast slowly over the fire. Behind her was a swamp of heavy grass and woods, but Patience felt secure with half a dozen soldiers for protection, as well as Miles, Papa, Thomas Trudgett—and Alf.

8

Cataraqui

Trudgett's prediction of a fair crossing held well on the second day. The wind had dropped and the oarsmen rowed steadily across the calm lake.

"We sail around that island and then down the channel to Cataraqui," Trudgett said to Papa. "I'll put the sergeant in charge of unloading and take you up to the fort. Major Ross is in command there. He rebuilt Fort Frontenac as well as the one we just left at Oswego. He's had his troubles both with Loyalists who want more than their share of supplies and with some of his own officers too, but he's a first-rate soldier and well respected by everyone. He'll look after you."

As the batteau passed the island a light breeze began to blow from the west.

"Hoist the sail!" Trudgett called, and the weary soldiers shipped oars. He turned back to Papa. "You won't be able to use the horses for this first winter," he said, "and you won't have feed for them, so I suggest you leave them with me at the fort. I'll see that they are properly cared for."

"Thank you, Tom. I knew we couldn't keep them and I dreaded the thought of selling them," Papa answered.

As he spoke Cataraqui came slowly into view.

"Don't be disappointed," Trudgett said to the disconsolate group sitting in the bow of the boat. "You can't expect Philadelphia. But," he added hopefully, "it is bigger and busier than Oswego." Mama laughed.

They disembarked at the wharf. Beyond lay ramshackle wooden houses, huts, and tents huddled around a fort. Soldiers on shore shouted to the crew. Townsfolk and settlers paused to inspect the new arrivals. A cart rattled by on the rutted dirt road that led up to the fort. There were many small boats tied along the wharf and pulled up on the rocky shore nearby. Some were being loaded with supplies to be taken back to settlers along the river.

"Miles, you and Alf help me take our belongings over there," Papa said, pointing to an open space above the road. "Abigail, you and Patience watch over them while we take the horses to the fort and report to Major Ross."

A dog with a long sausage in its mouth ran out of one of the houses, chased by a fat bald-headed man swinging a meat axe and swearing. The dog disappeared through the small crowd on the wharf.

"It's certainly lively here," said Mama, on whom all the activity had acted as a tonic.

"I've seen better places," Alf commented.

Fifteen minutes later Papa, Miles, Alf, and Thomas Trudgett led the horses up the slope to the fort. They wended their way through Quakers, Indians, Hessian soldiers, artisans, and bedraggled gentlemen. As they walked Trudgett pointed to some of the outlying buildings. "There are the stables and that's the King's Storehouse where you'll draw your supplies and a tent." He stopped a passing stable-boy and put Robin and Richard in his charge. "Give them some exercise, Danny, and a good rubdown afterwards. They've just come from Oswego."

Miles was reassured by the friendly way in which the boy talked to the horses and rubbed their necks before he took them away.

"I'll see that he dosses 'em down proper," said Alf and he walked away with the stable-boy before anyone could object.

"Now let's find Major Ross," said Trudgett, escorting Papa and Miles into the fort. He stopped at a door where a corporal lounged on guard. "I'd like to see Major Ross, corporal."

"Sorry, sir. The major left this morning. Took a small party north, sir. He'll be gone about a week he said, sir. Captain Castlevane is in command, sir."

The corporal had close-set eyes and a sly look. He seemed to enjoy telling Trudgett that Major Ross had gone and that Castlevane was now in charge.

After a hint of a pause, Trudgett said: "Very well, corporal, we'd like to see Captain Castlevane."

"Yes, sir. If you'd wait a moment, sir." The corporal opened the door and went inside.

"Send them in." They heard a haughty nasal voice.

The corporal opened the door to admit them. "Will this stream of threadbare Loyalists never end? Ah, Trudgett," said Castlevane as they stepped into the room. "What have you brought us this time?" He leaned back in his chair, propped his gleaming boots on the edge of a table, and gazed at the ceiling.

Trudgett stood at attention. "Captain James Avery of the Pennsylvania Loyalists and his family, requesting the land grant of the King for services rendered, sir."

There was a long silence and then Castlevane slowly swung his boots off the table and for the first time looked at the Averys.

"I am Captain Aubrey Castlevane. It is my duty to assist those who fought loyally for His Majesty. Your regiment, sir?"

"The Pennsylvania Loyalists," Papa replied.

"Yes." Castlevane dragged the word out. "That's what I thought Trudgett said. The Pennsylvania Loyalists were disbanded in New Brunswick in '83. You arrive from Oswego in '84. That's an odd way to travel from New Brunswick to Cataraqui, sir." His eyes narrowed and his lips curved in a false smile as he surveyed Papa.

"I did not travel north with my regiment and have not come from New Brunswick," said Papa, angered by Castlevane's insinuations. "I was left to recover from my wounds in Pensacola."

"Were the wounded not shipped to New York in '82?"

"Yes," said Papa stiffly, "but I took smallpox. Then a series of misadventures prevented me from rejoining my regiment."

Castlevane smiled coldly across the table. "Did the regiment leave you or did you leave the regiment? How do I know that you are not a deserter?"

"Sir," interrupted Trudgett.

"Be quiet, sir!" barked Castlevane. "I am in command here."

Papa took his parole paper from his pouch, carefully unfolded it, and laid it on the table. "That, sir, is my parole paper—an item that is not issued to deserters."

Castlevane picked up the paper and looked at it. "I can't read this mumbo-jumbo!"

"It's Spanish," said Miles indignantly.

Castlevane glared at him. "You read it then, cub," he said, and threw the paper across the table.

Miles flushed. "I can't," he mumbled.

"And you, Trudgett? Can you read Spanish or am I expected to believe the weird tale of a deserter?"

"Yes, sir," said Trudgett icily. He stepped forward, took the paper from Miles, and began to read.

"In the Name of the King. His Excellency the Governor of Pensacola hereby grants parole to James Avery, captain in the British forces. Signed by the seal of the Governor of Louisiana Bernardo de Galvez." Trudgett folded the parole paper, laid it on the table, and stepped back.

The room was very quiet. Castlevane sat furious, at a loss for words. It had not occurred to him that Trudgett might be able to read Spanish. "That's not much for all that scribbling," he spluttered. "It seems pretty suspicious to me."

"You have challenged my word," said Papa. "Are you about to dispute the word of your fellow officer as well? I require my land grant now. Winter is coming soon and I must prepare for it or my family will surely perish."

There was another silence. "Very well, Avery," Castlevane drawled, "but I do not consider this matter closed." He drummed his fingers on the table for a moment, then he opened a drawer and took out a small piece of paper. He scratched something out, wrote two words on it, then looked up with a half-smile.

"Your location ticket," he said. He threw the paper across the table. "You may hold this land on a temporary basis, pending clearance of your name. That will be all."

With a curt bow Papa picked up the ticket and the three of them left the fort and walked slowly towards the wharf.

When they were safely away from the fort, Miles turned to Trudgett. "What luck that you could read Spanish," he said. "That viper Castlevane had us at his mercy!"

Trudgett started to laugh and Miles felt wounded.

"It's all right, Miles," Trudgett said. "I'm not laughing at you. I can't read a word of Spanish. I think Castlevane suspected, but he couldn't be sure." He turned to Papa. "Let me see the land location. I don't like the way he smiled when he gave it to you." He stopped to study it while Miles and Papa waited anxiously. "I see why it appealed to him." Tom laughed. "It is a section known around here as Grimble's Plot. Grimble left in a hurry one day when a settler from Quebec recognized him. He's a notorious robber. No one has seen him since and of course his land was confiscated."

Miles was outraged. "He dishonours our name and then gives us the land of a thief! Papa, you must do something!"

"Enough, Miles," said Papa calmly. "This whole affair is a tempest in a teapot. Surviving the winter and preparing the land for spring crops must be our main concern. I know what I am and no arrogant English popinjay will disturb me."

"But the honour of our name is at stake!"

"Think of practical matters for a change. We're dealing with a petty tyrant who is merely a nuisance. We have land now and I'll write to Colonel Allen for my papers. When they arrive I'll have another word with the elegant captain." Papa smiled as if the thought pleased him. "Meanwhile we must find our land. How do we reach it, Tom?"

"By boat. Loyalists are usually transported by the army. However, it is late in the season and most of them are settled—"

"I'll ask no favours of Castlevane," said Papa. "We'll

build ourselves a raft, if necessary. It will be practice for building a house.''

"There's one already built," said Tom. "I saw it when we went there to hunt for Grimble. He had done almost no work on the land but he had built a hut, as Castlevane would have known if he'd ever deigned to set foot out of the officers' quarters. He thinks he's done you a bad turn because the plot is so remote and not on the river, but the land is good. And you have a fine neighbour too. His name is Simon Trick. He was a sergeant-major in the army, but his time was up and he decided to stay here with his wife and his boy, Sam.''

"That's good news," said Papa.

"And Miles," said Trudgett, "I must tell you that Grimble is rumoured to have left his plunder somewhere up there. The merchants of Montreal have offered a reward for Grimble and the return of the loot.''

"How much is the reward?" asked Miles.

"Now you are being more practical," said Papa.

Patience saw Miles and Papa and Tom approaching and ran eagerly towards them, her feet sending up little spurts of dust behind her.

"Where is our land? Is it near here?"

"Not exactly," said Papa slowly.

"It's the best land in the world, prattlebox," said Trudgett. He took Patience's arm and escorted her gallantly back to Mama who waited impatiently beside their baggage.

"What do we do now?" Mama asked. She drew her shawl more tightly around her, for a chill wind blew in from the lake.

"I'll take you to the storehouse for supplies," said Trudgett.

"Why did that cur treat us like criminals, Papa?" asked Miles as they carried their belongings over to the storehouse.

"I don't know for certain," said Papa, "but I could guess. Most of the British officers were insufferable boors who disliked and distrusted the Loyalists as much as they did the rebels. It may all become clearer soon," he added with a quick glance over his shoulder. "The corporal is following us."

"Cap'n, could ye spare a word?" said the corporal as he caught up to them. His eyes were sharp and greedy.

Papa stopped.

"Corporal Finlay, sir. I hates to see a good man like you get a rock pile in a swamp for a farm. Cap'n Castlevane was a mite hasty in his judgement up there, but something else can be arranged." His eyes darted about and he leaned closer to Papa. "But 'twould take a little time maybe, and," he coughed, "some money. Jewels and trinkets, they won't do you no good in the woods. I can have your name cleared and you'll get choice waterfront land with no questions asked."

Papa laid his hand on Finlay's shoulder and spoke very quietly. "Corporal, I was with a band of Indians once when a soldier, through lying and cheating, tried to deprive them of their rights."

Finlay struggled, but he couldn't escape the iron grip on his shoulder.

Papa continued: "Would you like to hear more of the fate of this liar and cheat?"

Finlay wriggled free and bolted back to the fort as though the devil was after him, nearly knocking over Alf as he ran.

"You have some trouble with the corporal, mate?" Alf asked Miles, taking one of the bags from him.

"That blackguard Castlevane is crooked as a corkscrew," Miles said.

"Captain Castlevane," Alf said slowly. "I've heard of 'im already today. Keep out of 'is way, they say. It's safer to step barefoot on a rattlesnake than to tangle with 'im."

By the time they reached the storehouse, Mama was on her way out, her arms filled.

"We have salt pork and peas and flour," she said excitedly. "Enough for the winter. And we've been given a little butter and seeds and an axe and a hoe."

Trudgett followed her, hidden in folds of canvas. "I'll help you set up this tent," he said.

Alf and Miles took it from him and followed Trudgett as he led them towards a spot where other small white tents lay scattered on the grass. After the tent had been put up Mama invited Tom to stay for dinner.

"We've had a taste of your army cooking," she said. "Now you must sample my cooking."

"After supper I shall write to the Governor in Quebec and the authorities in England for word of Honor," said Papa, "and to Colonel Allen in New Brunswick for verification of my story. Tom, you will forward the letters for me, won't you? I wouldn't care to entrust them to Castlevane. Now where is that soup you promised us, Abby, and where has that monkey Alf disappeared to again?"

"Reporting for duty, General," said Alf, coming towards them from the storehouse carrying a large cheese under one arm.

"Shouldn't you report in, lad?" Trudgett asked Alf after supper.

"Tomorrow," promised Alf. "Honest."

"You'd better do it now, or they might put you in Corporal Finlay's squad."

"Now there's a thought to ruin a good supper," said Alf. He quickly bid good night to everyone and hurried back to the fort.

"They wouldn't do that to Alf, would they?" asked Patience.

"Castlevane will if he finds out he's a friend of yours," said Trudgett. "But I'd worry more about Finlay than Alf in that case."

9

Grimble's Plot

Early next morning Trudgett called from outside the tent: "Time to get up! There's work to do!"

When they had all emerged from the tent into the brisk morning air, Trudgett said to Papa: "I gave your letters to a friend who is bound for Quebec, and now I'm off to Oswego. I want to say goodbye to you and wish you luck before I leave."

"But you just came from there," said Miles.

"Captain Castlevane feels very strongly that I should go straight back." Trudgett laughed.

"What happened to Alf?" asked Patience.

"I saw him as I left the fort. He's been given an important job to do—cleaning the stables for Corporal Finlay."

"This is terrible," said Mama. "Castlevane is victimizing you both for being our friends. Can't we do something, James?"

"Don't worry, Ma'am," said Trudgett. "There's nothing to do. It's just the army and much better that you don't get involved. That would give old Castlevane another shot at you, and you can rest assured that Alf and I can take care of ourselves."

"It sounds harsh but Tom is right, Abby," said Papa. "We'll add it to the slate and settle the score later. Meanwhile, let's walk down to the batteau with Tom and see him off."

"I'm sorry I couldn't arrange for your transportation as I had hoped. I tried."

"Never mind. We'll build a raft, though we can ill afford the time. I wish we could buy one."

"We can," said Mama. Her voice was unexpectedly determined as she rummaged in her bag. "There," she said. Triumphantly she handed Papa her silver spoons. "I knew I was right to bring them."

"My dear Abby," he protested. "This is not necessary."
"Oh yes it is."

When they reached the wharf Trudgett shook hands with Miles and Papa and kissed Patience and Mama on the cheek. Then he jumped on board the batteau and ordered the crew to cast off. The batteau moved slowly and steadily into the channel and disappeared in the mist that blanketed the lake.

Despite the bustling activity around him, Miles felt alone. He looked at Patience and saw that she was crying as she still waved vigorously at the batteau.

"None of this," said Papa, wiping her tears with his sleeve. "No more moping, now. We'll soon be off to our land."

They did trade most of the spoons for a small batteau and that afternoon they loaded their supplies on board. There was a fair wind from the north-east and they departed under sail.

"I trust this will be our last journey," said Mama. "Unless it's to find Honor," she added. "I'd go to the ends of the earth for that."

"I'm sick of travelling," said Patience. However, her interest revived when she saw Miles steering the batteau. "I want a turn," she said. "Miles is having all the fun."

"What green eyes you have," said Papa. "Let her try it then, Miles. But be careful, Patience."

Delighted, she took the steering oar from her brother. They scudded along before the wind, past a shoreline that bristled with trees and green firs.

"I'm Christopher Columbus and I'm about to discover America," Patience said dreamily.

"You're a blockhead and you're about to discover how to be shipwrecked!" said Papa grabbing the oar, for the batteau was heading straight for a rock.

In the late afternoon the wind dropped. Papa and Miles took turns rowing the clumsy little boat. Every half hour they stopped to rest. Then, when it began to grow dark, they beached the batteau and built a big fire on the rocky shore. The night air was sharp and cold.

"This is an ague-and-fever evening," said Papa. "The winter is harsher here than in Philadelphia. We'll reach our hut only in the nick of time." They listened to the wind in the branches of the trees. And then they heard something else: a frightening, lonely cry of torment. Wolves!

"Pile up the fire," Papa ordered. They threw on more branches, but they had not had time to gather much wood. As the fire burned higher their supply of wood grew low. The howls came closer.

"They are coming our way," said Papa. "Get into the batteau."

The three of them scrambled into the boat and Papa, wading into the frigid water, shoved it offshore and clambered in himself. Miles looked back just as the first grey shadow moved across the light of the fire. It sniffed where they had been sitting and then howled.

Papa rowed the boat well away from the shore out into the safety of the lake. Miles wrapped his army blanket around Patience and they both shivered as they peered back at the grey ghost by the fire.

The Averys spent a miserable night on the dark water. At daybreak they went cautiously ashore and built a small fire. They boiled some water and Mama made gruel for breakfast. Then they wearily set off again.

"When will we ever get there?" Patience said as they continued on past more and more tree-lined shores. But when at last, late in the afternoon, they came to a small cove and Papa steered the batteau into it, she was surprised. "It looks like all the others," she said. "Nothing but trees. How do you know that it's the right one?"

Papa tied the batteau to a tree without answering. "Sometimes when I listen to Patience," he observed to Mama as he helped her ashore, "I feel like Robinson Crusoe. We too have a parrot to chatter at us in the wilderness."

"You are too harsh with the child," said Mama. "How *do* you know that this is the right spot?"

"Now don't you start too," said Papa. "According to the map Tom sketched for me this land belongs to our neighbour, Simon Trick. We must walk further inland to find ours."

Miles pointed to a log house standing on top of a low hill, the first real settler's house they had seen.

"It's not much like Quince Alley," Mama said.

"We must call upon our neighbours," said Papa. After they had unloaded their belongings, he began to climb the little hill and the others followed.

"Look, there's Sam Trick," said Miles. A boy with shaggy

red hair streaked across the clearing and into the house.

"An odd cub," said Papa. "Let us hope his parents are more mannerly." He knocked on the door.

The man who answered was so tall and broad that he filled the doorway. His iron-grey hair was tied back with a strip of deerskin and he had bushy black eyebrows that met over his nose. He bowed to Mama and gave Patience a friendly look from piercing brown eyes.

Papa introduced himself: "I am James Avery and this is my wife Abigail and our children Miles and Patience. We've been given Grimble's Plot."

"Maggie, meet our new neighbours," Mr Trick called over his shoulder without ceremony.

"Come and set down," Mrs Trick said, waving a spoon welcomingly at them. She spoke in a Scottish brogue as thick as porridge.

She was short and fat and had at least three chins and black twinkling eyes like currants in a bun. She wore moccasins and a deerskin skirt, topped with a fringed purple shawl. Above it all, flaming brightly, was a mop of red curls. "She's wearing a wig!" Patience whispered to Miles as the Averys entered the cabin, following the delicious smell that came from a large pot on the fire.

"Stay the night," Mrs Trick said hospitably. "Stay the week. Sam needs young company. He's gone as shy as a ground squirrel since we've been here, and he's no more manners than a bear." She gave Sam, who squatted silently by the fire, a friendly whack on the head with her spoon.

"That's very kind of you," said Papa, "but we are anxious to reach our land before it grows too dark."

"Don't push the folks around before they've even settled in," Mr Trick protested. "They'll want to see their house."

"Very well. But at least take this with you." She pulled a loaf of bread out of the fireplace. "Sammy will lead you over the trail."

Papa thanked her, and the Averys reluctantly left the warmth of the house. They walked in single file under the rustling trees, for the trail was narrow.

Sam moved ahead of them and Miles stumbled hurriedly along the uneven path to join him.

"How long have you been here?" he asked. "Do you like it?"

Swish! Miles jumped back, startled, as an overhanging branch released by Sam swept past his nose.

"Where were you before?" he asked, louder this time. Sam ignored him.

"All right, you bumpkin!" said Miles. He stopped hurrying and fell back. He concentrated on trying to remember every turn in the trail but soon had to give up. He felt hopelessly lost. Finally Sam stopped and pointed. One by one the tired Averys dragged their bundles, their bags, and themselves into a small clearing. In the dim light they saw a log house surrounded by tree stumps.

"Let's hope Grimble was as good a carpenter as he was a thief," said Papa. Taking the rushlight that Mrs Trick had given him, he stepped into their new home. Patience stumbled after him. Miles looked around for Sam Trick, but he was already heading back.

When Papa held the light aloft, they could see that the house was very small and had no windows. The ill-fitting door was made of a set of logs clumsily fastened together. The only furniture they saw in the sputtering light was a large tree-stump table in the middle of the dirt floor and a huge bed. Miles found that it was made with poles wedged into the rough logs of the wall, supported by posts driven into the earth. A rough canvas covering stuffed with dried grass, moss, and withered leaves served as a mattress. It rustled and crackled when he sat on it.

Papa lit a fire in the fireplace and said: "We'll be snug as pokers here."

Mama had brought an iron kettle from Cataraqui and they all gathered around the fire to make tea, and to toast Mrs Trick's bread. The logs crackled cheerily, drowning out the wind that whistled through the nooks and crannies of the house.

After supper Mama spread their blankets on Grimble's big bed and Papa built up the fire, while Miles brought in wood for the morning.

"Will that be enough?" he asked as he carried in a third load, but there was no sound from the big bed—the others were fast asleep. He threw an extra log on the fire and watched the flames. "I'm a long way from becoming a British officer now," he thought.

10

Supper with the Tricks

Patience rolled over on her back and opened her eyes. The blackness above was cracked in a few places where Papa would have to mend the roof. She was all alone in the middle of the bed so she could stretch her arms and legs, but she could not touch the end or the sides. She turned to look at the hut walls. In the darkness they were black with thin white lines of light running along the length of the room.

She heard Miles' voice outside. "Is Patience ever going to wake up?"

"Let her sleep awhile yet," said Mama. "We won't breakfast until Papa comes back."

Patience threw off the blanket, stepped on the cold dirt floor, and skipped quickly over to the fireplace to put on her clothes. She took down a fox skin that hung on a peg on the wall by the fire and put it around her neck. Stroking the long fur, she went over to the door and peered through the spaces between the logs. Miles came into view carrying a kettle of water, which he had filled at the stream that ran near one side of the clearing.

Patience quickly put a bag on the bed, threw the blanket over it, and ran back to stand flat against the wall next to the door.

It opened and Miles stepped inside. He looked over at the form on the bed, then he set the kettle down. Patience watched from behind the door as he picked up a tin cup from the table, dipped it in the kettle, and crept towards the bed. Just as he raised the cup to empty it over the huddled figure, Patience threw the fox fur around his neck, hissed like a wild cat, and dug her nails into his back. Then she fled from the hut, while Miles tore at the wild beast that had clawed at him in the darkness.

Patience sat down beside Mama in the warm sun.

"What's happening in there?" asked Mama.

Miles emerged, with water dripping from his chin, his shirt soaked, and a fox fur in his hands.

"What happened to you, Miles?" Mama asked.

"Miles has just fought a wildcat bare-handed. It happens all the time in Canada," Patience said.

Miles let out a roar and rushed at her. Patience darted around the tree stumps with Miles in hot pursuit. Then she jumped up on top of a broad stump and crowed: "I'm King George in his castle, And you're a rebel rascal!" As Miles reached for her, she jumped off and raced back to Mama.

Miles squatted down in front of them, panting and laughing.

Patience rubbed her right foot. "It hurts. There are sharp branches in the grass." She stared in surprise at Miles' feet. "You're wearing moccasins!"

"They aren't proper moccasins. I found some pieces of deerskin in the house and wrapped two of them around my feet. The fur keeps them nice and warm; the hide keeps them dry. They're much better than shoes."

"I want a pair."

"I'll make you some," he said and they went into the house together. Patience stood still while Miles wrapped two pieces of deerskin around her ankles and tied them with strips of hide.

"I never thought to be a cobbler," he said, watching her caper about the room. Then Mama came in, admired his handiwork, and insisted that she too must have a pair.

"I am sick of hobbling about," she said, lifting her skirt and looking at her worn shoes with displeasure. "Your efforts are hardly elegant, Miles, but perhaps they will keep us warm. Where did you find the deerskins?"

"In one of those sacks," said Miles. "I was hoping to find Grimble's loot that Thomas talked about."

They investigated the sacks in the corner and Mama said their contents would be more useful than any treasure hoard.

"We can't wear gold," she said, "but with these blankets I shall turn seamstress again and make warm coats. And the skins will make shoes and petticoats and breeches."

There was a rustling at the door.

"Grimble!" shrieked Patience. But it was only Mr Trick who loomed in the doorway.

"Malachi won't be back," he chuckled. "He's probably robbed his way to Quebec by now. What a piece of mischief he was. I came to show you the property," he said to Papa who had followed him in. "Shall we walk around it together?"

"Will you be all right, Abby?" Papa asked. "Stay in the clearing and nothing will harm you."

"Did Sam come with you?" Miles asked.

Mr Trick knotted his eyebrows and hummed a tune. "He seemed to be off somewhere when I left," he said.

After the men had gone, taking Miles with them, Mama sat down on the bed and sighed as she looked around her new house.

"Well, Patience," she said, "we must begin to set things to rights."

"What do you have in the bag, Mama?" asked Patience. "Aren't you going to unpack it?"

"It seems so foolish now," said Mama, and she looked around the bare smoky room. "Only a few of Papa's favourite books, and some seeds for a garden, and the rest of my silver spoons, and—oh, I don't know. What a fribble I was, to be sure!" She shook her head impatiently and rose, saying to Patience: "Papa would rather teach than cut down trees, but he is not complaining, nor must I. Let us put out his books for him as a surprise, and then, since we have no bake-oven, I shall try to bake bread in the fireplace. I noticed yesterday that Mrs Trick did it that way."

She unwrapped the clock and stood it on a wooden shelf beside the fireplace. It ticked cheerfully as if it had never left Philadelphia and been joggled across streams and woods on horseback for hundreds of miles.

Patience arranged Papa's books carefully beside the clock. She was glad to see some that she hadn't read and recited their titles: *Paradise Lost*, *Addison's Essays*, *Gulliver's Travels*, *The Plays of William Shakespeare*. She unpacked her own well-thumbed volumes—including *Goody Two-Shoes*, *The Governess*, and *Christmas Tales*—and arranged them on the other side. Then she hung her squashed bonnet on one of the wooden pegs and went to help Mama with the bread.

Unfortunately the bread-making was not a success. When the others came back they found Mama in tears by the fire. A charred loaf was lying on the floor.

"Is your wife lonely already?" asked Mr Trick with surprise.

"No," said Patience. "It is because we are out of bread. We have flour, but Mama does not understand how to bake bread without an oven."

"Well," said Mr Trick twitching his eyebrows, "if that's all, I have a remedy. You must come to take potluck with us this evening, and after dinner Maggie will show you how to make bread. I'll be off now, but mind you come before dark."

Later, when they saw the Tricks' house again, they looked at it with much more respect.

"I wish we had a loft and a root cellar and oiled-paper windows," said Mama.

"And a nice plank door!" said Papa knocking. It opened and Mr Trick beamed a welcome from under his eyebrows.

Potluck supper turned out to be porcupine (it tasted like roast pork), pumpkin bread, and nuts and wine.

"Did you make the wine too?" asked Mama.

"Oh, we can make liquor to sweeten our lips, Of pumpkins, of parsnips, of walnut-tree chips," sang Mr Trick. "So much fruit grows in these woods that next year we shall have a cellar of wines more fit for glittering Nabobs from India than humble settlers in the Cataraqui woods. Won't we, my dear old Scotch mope?" He stretched one arm around his wife's broad waist.

"Where is Sam?" asked Miles. Mr Trick shook his head at his wife, but her face grew nearly as red as her hair and she said defiantly: "No, Simon, I won't be quiet." She turned to the Averys. "Sammy's that shy with proper folks, but he's always rambling about the woods with them Mississagys."

"What are Mississagys?" Patience asked.

"Half-naked savages."

"Now, Margaret," said Mr Trick. "He's learned some handy lessons from the Indians. We wouldn't have had near as many salmon dinners without that knack of his of spearing 'em with a stick. He's promised me some maskinonge when the ice-fishing starts—and a tasty snack they make."

"'Tisn't natural," grumbled Mrs Trick, "careering through the woods all day, as wild as a buck."

"Doesn't he want to play with us?" asked Patience, intrigued by this strange boy who wandered with the Indians.

"Give the lad time," said Mr Trick.

Miles muttered: "Let him prate for pigeons."

After dinner Patience insisted that Papa tell the Tricks the story of the shipwreck. Mama talked of Philadelphia and why they had come to Canada, and told them about Honor.

Mrs Trick shed a tear when Mama described leaving the house in Quince Alley. She hugged Patience, gave her a honeycomb, and explained that her family had been driven away from the Scottish Highlands when she was only a child. The Averys' story had brought back sad memories of her father shot, a house burned, and of being hunted down by English soldiers.

"But," Patience said, "Mr Trick was an English soldier. How could you marry him?"

"Patience!" said Mama.

"Don't scold her," said Mrs Trick. "I met Simon years later when I was grown up and learned that soldiers are only men, with all the good and the bad of ordinary men until war comes. War turns men into wild beasts, both good men and bad. Wars is fit for kings and fools. Kings make wars and fools fight 'em.''

Miles couldn't hold his tongue any longer. "What of the bravery of men fighting for their king, and God?''

"All foolishness. How often is the fight for someone else's country, the king is a rogue or a simpleton, and both sides claim God?''

"What about—''

"Quiet now, Miles," Mama said. "There will be other nights to talk. We must go. Mrs Trick, thank you for a fine meal.''

Mr Trick gave them each a pine-knot for a light before they set out for home. "Don't set yourselves on fire," he warned.

Stumbling along the humpy trail, Patience gazed at the swaying tree tops against the sky. She pulled Miles' arm. "Look at the black banners in the night," she said.

"I like Mrs Trick," Mama told Papa, "but I'm shocked to death at having a Jacobite for a neighbour. All that talk of Bonnie Prince Charlie and the-King-over-the-water, and before the children too.''

Papa stopped in the middle of the path. "Nonsense! I am as loyal to King George as any man, but there must be freedom for all to speak as they will, whether or not we like what they say. What kind of freedom leaves no room for honest dissent? As we know full well, the Americans boast of freedom as if they had invented it, but only rebels are welcome there now." He brandished his torch dangerously near Mama's head in his excitement.

Mama laughed. "James, I do believe they make good wine in these parts." She began to sing a marching song and they tramped merrily home.

11

Visitors

During October both Mr and Mrs Trick came over frequently. They had been settled on their land for nearly two years and were well used to life in the woods.

"You can sow some seed now and it will set all winter under the snow." Mr Trick liked giving advice. "But you'll need to clear more land for the spring. You must burn the underbrush, chop down all the trees you can, and split rails to build a fence to keep animals out. It's best to make it five or six feet high."

"When I think of all these trees to be cut and burned I feel like taking up Grimble's trade," said Papa.

"That Grimble was a sloppy workman." Mr Trick shook his head as he gazed around at the tree trunks that lay scattered on the Averys' clearing. Suddenly he broke into a grin and slapped Papa's back. "At least there will be no time to get lonely," he said. "There's work enough here to keep you all as busy as bees. Maggie and I will do what we can to help. Not our Sammy though, I fear."

Day by day Papa and Miles dragged the smaller trees

together and chopped the big ones into manageable lengths for burning. The axe they had been given at the fort was not much heavier than a hatchet and it was slow, gruelling work. They seemed to make little progress.

Sometimes they went hunting. "Salt pork and peas are all very well," Papa told Mama after one excursion when he and Miles had shot a deer, "but we'll enjoy this come winter."

Mr Trick showed Miles how to dig a small root cellar for their stores and Mrs Trick gave them some pumpkins and squash to put in it. She took Mama and Patience for long walks in the woods and showed them all the roots and berries they could eat.

"There's cranberries in the marshes," she told them enthusiastically one afternoon as they explored. "Wild strawberries and raspberries in the summer. There's honey from wild bees for sweetening; sumach flowers and boiling water will make lemonade for Miss Patience and sassafras leaves will make tea for Mrs Avery. There's wild plums, cherries, and crabapples too. I makes squirrel soup or pie once a week and Simon likes a nice bit o' salmon or a piece of eel pie. My Sammy likes pigeon pasties best. Them birds roosts in the trees by the hundreds. Why, they're so tame they walks about and lets you hit 'em on the head with a stick.

"I boils chestnuts and hickories and corn to make milk since we don't have a cow yet and—"

"Stop, stop!" Mama protested, laughing. "You make the woods sound like a storehouse for kings."

"Medicines too," continued Mrs Trick with a fanatical gleam in her eye. As if checking a list, she counted on her fingers and began to recite.

"There's catnip tea for stomach-ache or bad chests, tansy tea for indigestion—"

"We'll surely need that," interrupted Mama.

"Cherry bark for the blood; for scalds and burns, black alder lard, resin, and beeswax; smartweed steeped in vinegar for Sammy's bruises; mandrake to gargle and ginseng for being in the dumps or old age. Oh, and tacamahac leaves for healing wounds," she added, anxious not to forget anything.

"A wilderness apothecary shop," said Mama. "Now, will you come and have a cup of China tea and show us how to make a broom?"

Despite Mrs Trick's willing assistance, Mama and Patience found housekeeping in the hut difficult and exhausting. There was no furniture to polish or china to wash and no trips to the market as in Quince Alley. Instead there was a dirt floor to be endlessly swept and kept tidy, meat to be hacked into strips and dried, nuts to be gathered, and the fire to be watched and fed constantly.

Mrs Trick taught Mama how to make thread from the basswood trees—a necessity, for their already shabby clothes were quickly becoming torn to pieces from the rough work and the bramble-strewn woods. Mama and Patience spent long hours trying to get the clothes clean by pounding them on the rocks in the cold spring water.

Once their small supply of flour had been used, Mama was forced to make her own. Milling the grain took hours of her time. Miles had found a hollowed-out stump that Mr Trick told them could be used for grinding their wheat into rough flour. Mr Trick showed Mama how to put the wheat inside the stump and hit it with a heavy pounder. Mama always had to lie down after she did this. Then, too soon, it was time to be up again to bake and mend. She began to look worn and tired.

Patience was kept busy hunting for nuts and the pine-knots that they used to light the dark windowless hut. They had no tallow or grease to make candles.

"I feel like a squirrel preparing for winter," she would grumble as she sorted nuts and carried them to the root cellar in birch baskets. She also collected armloads of twigs for the fire, and moss to chink the spaces in the hut. She enjoyed gathering the fresh cedar branches that Mama scattered on the floor every day to keep the air sweet in the small stuffy house.

It was always late in the afternoon before she and Miles were free to play stump tag or slide gloriously and muddily down the hill on pieces of birchbark.

The sun set earlier each day and the nights grew longer. The family no longer fell into bed directly after supper, exhausted by the day's work. Papa began to make furniture by the light of the pine-knots and the fire. He made two narrow beds for Miles and Patience and put them against the walls near the fire. Then he started to make stools to sit on at the tree-stump table.

Mama stopped trying vainly to make the hut look like the house on Quince Alley and began to take an interest in new chores. She stuffed two sacks with moss and leaves for mattresses. When that was done, she measured both Papa and Miles for deerskin breeches and jackets. "We'll have skirts too," she promised Patience, "just like Mrs Trick."

"And a purple shawl and a red wig?" Patience asked hopefully.

One day when Patience was collecting moss at the edge of the clearing, she saw a group of men filing through the woods. At first she thought they were British soldiers because some of them had red coats and laced hats, but when they came nearer she saw that they also wore deerskin trousers and had long black pigtails. Those who didn't have hats wore scarlet and blue feathers in their hair.

She ran to the house to tell Miles and Mama. (Papa had gone hunting with Mr Trick.)

"Don't be frightened," said Mama in an unsteady voice. "The Indians here are supposed to be friendly. We'll stay in the house and maybe they will go away."

They waited, listening to the ticking clock. Suddenly the door opened and eight Indians marched into the house with slow and dignified steps. They filled the room, so that Miles and Patience and Mama had to press against the wall.

The Indians looked around the room curiously, talking loudly to each other. Several turned the pages of the books with great interest and one of them was especially pleased by the clock. He held it to his ear, shook it, and then set it gently down again upon the shelf.

"Bostonese?" said one Indian, resplendent in scarlet cloak and eagle feathers, his face painted with chalky circles. "Cataraqui?"

"Yes, yes—Cataraqui," Mama answered uneasily.

The Indians then looked around the room one last time and, still talking among themselves, filed out.

The three Averys watched them disappear into the woods.

"Miles! Look there!" Patience said, as a red head appeared and disappeared among the trees. "It's Sam Trick. Those must be his Mississagys!"

That night as they ate their supper of wild turkey, Mama pushed away her untouched plate and said: "I think I will lie down. I seem to have a squeamish stomach after today's adventure."

Papa felt her forehead. "Into bed with you," he said. "You have a raging fever."

Shortly afterwards Mama was moaning and tossing about on the bed.

"I must go for Mrs Trick," Papa said. "She has some knowledge of physic. Patience, watch over your mother till I return. Miles, you see to the fire and be sure that there is wood enough to last until morning. There is a wind to freeze the blood tonight."

Miles and Patience sat in unhappy silence after he had left.

"I'm going out for more wood," Miles said.

"Don't go."

"You heard what Papa said. I won't be long." Whistling loudly to convince Patience and himself that he was unafraid, Miles went out into the windy darkness. Patience sat shivering by the fire. The clock ticked, the fire crackled, the wind outside howled.

Suddenly Mama cried out. "Honor! Sally!" Patience ran to her, but Mama looked at her unseeingly. "Honor?"

"No, Mama, it's Patience. Don't you know me?"

Mama muttered to herself and kicked off the blankets. Patience put them on again and felt her head. It was burning hot. "Where is Miles? Oh, what can I do?" Then she remembered how Mama used to bathe her forehead and face when she was feverish. She ran for the kettle, but it was empty.

"Miles will have to get water from the spring as soon as he comes back." She made a fan from a piece of bark and fanned Mama. This seemed to soothe her for a few minutes, but she became restless again and more feverish than ever. "I must get water."

Patience wrapped a shawl around her shoulders and picked up the kettle. The wind blew the door open when she unlatched it and she had to struggle to get it closed behind her. She ran as fast as she could in the dark with the kettle banging against her legs. Past strange shapes she tore, stumbling on ground made unfamiliar by the night. As she reached the stream she slipped and dropped the kettle, which clanged away out of reach. She waded into the icy water and found it jammed between two rocks.

"Miles, help me, Miles!" she cried. "Help!" Her cry was lost in the wind. She pulled again at the kettle but it was immovable. Her feet were numb, her fingers ached. "Help!"

She heard a movement in the darkness. Half-blinded by tears she looked hopelessly around. "Miles?" she quavered, abandoning the kettle and struggling out of the water. "Miles?"

A dark shape advanced towards her. "Miles?" she said again hoarsely, backing away.

Out of the darkness came a quiet and reassuring voice: "It's only me, Sam Trick."

Patience took one look at Sam and burst into violent sobs of relief.

"Don't cry. I didn't mean to frighten you, honestly." Patience sobbed on. "What's the matter?"

"The kettle's stuck and Mama's very sick and I must get back to her."

Sam freed the kettle, filled it, then took Patience's hand and led her gently towards the hut.

As they approached the door they heard cries from the woodpile.

"Is that you, Miles?" Patience cried. "Sam, will you find him while I see to Mama?"

"I'll find him." Sam took the kettle into the house and went back out into the wind.

The woodpile loomed up in the darkness.

"Patience, I'm over here." There was an odd quaver in Miles' voice. "Be careful or you'll pull the rest down on top of me."

"Be careful yourself," said Sam, lifting the logs that pinned Miles' leg to the ground. "Lie still and I'll get you out. Is it broken?"

"It must be. Can you help me to the house? I'm freezing."

Without answering, Sam helped Miles to his feet and half lifted, half carried him back to the house.

Miles grimaced, grateful that the darkness concealed the tears of pain on his cheeks.

"Here's your next patient," Sam announced after he had pushed the door open and dumped Miles inside by the fire.

Sam examined Miles' leg. "No break there," he said. "It's just a wrenched knee. Wrap a cold wet cloth around it and it won't swell too much. And you'd better let your sister get the wood for the fire from now on. It's dangerous work."

"You smirking plough-jogger!" shouted Miles. "You save that talk until I can catch you!"

"Stop it!" said Patience. "You'll wake Mama and she's really sick. Sam, please bring us some wood. And will you stay until Papa comes back? He's gone for your mother."

"My mother!" cried Sam. Hastily he went out to get the wood.

"He lugged me along like a sack of meal," said Miles. "I'm all bruised and battered by that lummox."

"What happened?"

"The log pile fell on my leg. I called but you didn't come. Can you bring me some water?"

"Leave some for Mama. I had to go out in the dark for it, and I fell down and got hurt too, but then Sam came and helped me. He's nice, Miles. He's just shy, like a deer."

A sudden hail of blows attacked the door.

"Now your timid deer's trying to kick the door down," said Miles. When Patience opened it Sam struggled in under a load of wood.

Patience bathed Mama with water until she became cooler, and made her drink some tea. Sam sat cross-legged by the fire watching.

"Dear child," smiled Mama and she fell asleep. Patience wondered if she still thought that she was Honor. Then she and Miles took turns watching the fire until at last they heard voices.

Papa came in, followed by Mrs Trick. Without stopping to take off the army cape that she had flung over her shoulders, Mrs Trick went to Mama. She touched her forehead and uttered a satisfied grunt.

"She'll be on her legs soon enough," she said, diving into her bag. "But you must build up her strength with this and this and this." She put several small evil-coloured bottles on the stump-table. "Now for some tea! Then off to sleep, everyone. I can't have a whole pack of feverish—Sammy! What are *you* up to?"

There was no answer. Papa looked in bewilderment at Miles, clutching a wet rag to his knee, and at Patience whose face was scratched. "I leave an ailing wife and two healthy children and come home to find two survivors of the wars. What have you been doing?"

"Nothing," they chorused.

12

Sam Talks

"And why did your poor Mama take a fever so quick, do you suppose?" Mrs Trick demanded of the Averys next morning as she hammered in a peg for a horseshoe over the door. "D'ye have any enemies? It could be a witch, you know, casting a spell upon her.

" 'Tis at times like this," she continued dreamily, "that I long for a cow. Then the cure would be so simple. Just plunge a red-hot poker into a dish of cream ready to be churned and your Mama would be as fit as a fiddle in no time at all. Howsomever, we'll have to make do with what we have."

Under Mrs Trick's care Mama began to look well again in a day or so.

"It was the wormwood tea that cured her," said Patience, making a face.

"Maybe it was the eel broth," said Miles, "or the slippery elm jelly."

" 'Twas the horseshoe she hung over the door to protect

the house from evil," said Papa. Miles and Patience looked at him in surprise.

"You said yesterday that it was foolish superstition," Patience reminded him.

"Did I indeed? Well, to tell the truth, I don't care if Mrs Trick hangs a horse over the door as long as she makes Mama well again."

That afternoon Miles and Patience went in search of roots for Mrs Trick. It was snowing lightly and they exulted in the swirling flakes that washed their faces. "There's some yellow fungus," Miles said. "It's just the thing for Mrs Trick. Let's take it home."

"Let's not," said Patience. "She'll make us eat it."

"She's a fine cook as long as you're not sick. I'd like to be thrown into one of her strawberry pies as big as Lake Ontario and eat my way out!"

Their dessert at supper was pumpkin pudding, not strawberry pie. As they sat around the fire when they had finished eating they could hear wolf howls in the distance. A faraway expression came over Mrs Trick's plump face.

"Just listen to them witches' horses," she said.

"What do you mean?"

"Them howling wolves remind me of a story my Grandmother Grant told me," Mrs Trick continued, staring into the fire as if she saw pictures in it. "Seventh son of a seventh son, her father was. 'Twas said that she had the gift of the second sight from him. Born on Hallowe'en she was too. Some whispered that she was a witch."

"Was she?" Miles asked.

"No-o," said Mrs Trick. "But strange things did keep happening to her. She used to tell them to me when I was no bigger than you. I mind the time..."

She poked the fire and watched the flames disappearing like dancing blue elves. When she spoke again there was a lilting note in her voice that sounded like the ballads Mama used to sing to them.

"'Twas on a summer afternoon when she was being courted by my grandfather. She'd promised to meet him by the burn that flowed through the park around the clan chief's house. She was a tacksman's daughter and lived nearby. She'd stuck a white rose in her long red hair, and well pleased she was as she ran through the flowering woods to meet her Willie. She thought she'd never seen the sky so beautiful nor heard the birds singing so loud and sweet. But when she came to the old oak, a hush fell on the forest, and the darkness came on so sudden she feared she'd lose her way. She stopped then, afraid, for she saw something before her on the path like a grey fog. But the fog cleared and 'twas the clan chief's daughter, who'd run away a year ago in the night with Dugal Campbell of Clunas, him they called the Black. She and my grandmother had played together as children, and when Grandmother saw her in her fine white gown and kirtle of scarlet with her long hair streaming down her back like a golden fleece, she ran to her and caught her by the hand. But there was nothing there!

"Then my grandmother saw her again in the distance and she cried aloud: 'What is it? Why do you weep so sore and say not a word?' 'Bury my bones,' said the lady, and she pointed to the oak tree. 'Bury my bones!' And then she vanished."

"Oh!" said Patience. "Was she a ghost?"

"Ay," said Mrs Trick sadly. "My grandmother ran to the burn for my grandfather and sent him for a spade. He asked no questions when he saw what had happened to her."

"What had happened?"

"Her beautiful red hair, just like mine she always said it was, had turned as white as the rose she wore."

"Did he find any bones?" asked Miles.

"Yes, under the oak. They brought them to be buried in the churchyard. Dugal the Black had wooed and murdered her to be revenged in a family quarrel."

Mrs Trick sighed heavily and rose to put on the kettle for a bedtime cup of herb tea for Mama.

Next morning she decided that the time had come for her to leave. "With young Patience here you don't need me now," she told Mama. "Don't forget to carry a potato in your pocket to keep away the rheumatiz. I've left plenty of wormwood tea if you feel wobbly."

Just then Sam arrived to see his mother.

"Patience and Miles told me of how you saved us all, Sam," said Mama. "Thank you. I hope we will see you more often, though not in such dramatic circumstances."

Sam flushed red.

"I'm going home now, Sammy," said Mrs Trick, enveloping herself in the army cape. "But I'll walk on ahead." She winked at Patience. "You bide a bit with Miles and Patience. Perhaps some of their friendly ways will rub off on you."

The Averys thanked Mrs Trick again and waved her goodbye, promising to ta' care and follow her advice.

"Where do you go when you disappear into the woods?" Patience asked Sam when his mother had left.

"Around and about," he said.

"What do you do?"

"Oh, this and that, I have to go now." He nodded awkwardly to everyone and departed.

"He doesn't say much, does he?" said Mama.

"I'm going after him," said Miles. "Perhaps he'll be more friendly in his own territory."

He shivered when he opened the door, for despite the sun shining in the harsh blue sky, the air was cold.

He set off at a run, following the red head that bobbed in the distance. Walking was difficult, but he stumbled on, determined to keep up. Unaccustomed to the snow, he fell into a drift, and when he stood up Sam had disappeared.

"I'll follow his tracks," thought Miles. "I'll prove I know the woods as well as any bumpkin."

Even when the tracks veered away from the trail, Miles followed them doggedly. The snowflakes were now falling heavily. His foot slipped, there was a crack, and Miles lurched into two inches of freezing water.

"Blast him!" Crossly he squelched on, squinting from the glare of the snow as he looked for footprints.

Sam seemed intent on travelling in some strange path of his own making, through a cranberry bog and a cedar swamp, a grey mournful place that made Miles think of Mrs Trick's ghost story. Sometimes he thought he saw a flash of red through the trees, and then he would be left again with nothing but the endlessly sifting snow and the half-hidden prints.

He followed Sam's trail to a small clearing and stopped in bewilderment. It was filled with footprints!

"A pox on you, Sam Trick!" he called. A snowball hit him on the back of the head. He wheeled around angrily. "Stop skulking about like a spy. Come out and fight honestly!" Another snowball hit his head, and as Miles spun around snowballs pelted him faster and faster from all sides of the clearing.

Miles turned back for what he hoped was home, but he could not tell which of the dark pathways led to the real trail.

"I can't be lost," Miles thought, fighting a growing certainty that he was. "I *won't* be lost!" He sat down under a tree to think. A large mound of fresh snow fell on his head.

"Give up?" The voice came from above. Spluttering and brushing the snow from his hair, Miles peered up through the branches and saw Sam's face.

"Come down, you—you rattle-head!" he said. "Where did all those snowballs come from?"

"Fooled you, didn't we?" laughed Sam, slithering down the tree. "The Mississagys like to tease."

"You mean you had Indians throwing snowballs at me?"

"'Twas only a joke," said Sam. "I'm surprised. I never thought you'd get this far, a city boy like you. Come on, I'll take you home."

"Take yourself home!" roared Miles, refreshed by rage, and he leaped upon Sam. They became a squirming tangle of arms and legs as they rolled and bumped in the snow. The fight ended as quickly as it had begun when they hit a tree trunk.

"I'll take you hunting tomorrow if you like," Sam said unexpectedly.

Miles' nose was bleeding and Sam gave him a handful of snow to wipe it off. "What time do we leave?" Miles asked.

As he followed Sam home, with snow still trickling down his neck, Miles knew that their friendship had begun. His only regret was that the Mississagys had vanished before he could meet them. Sam promised to take him to their encampment.

"My friends are called Wawatam and Musinigon. You mustn't ask them their names. It's bad manners. They're afraid it will stunt their growth if they tell you."

"Is there anything else I should know?" asked Miles,

following faithfully in Sam's footsteps as he made his way unerringly through the forest. "Is that why you kept away from us, because you thought we'd call you Sam and you'd be a dwarf?"

"I shall be six feet two, just like my father," said Sam. "You must be careful never to point your finger at the moon, for the Mississagys think she will consider it an insult and that she will bite it off."

"Do they hunt with a bow and arrow?" asked Miles.

"They use guns mostly now," said Sam. "And it makes hunting harder. The old men say that the animals were much tamer before. The hunters use charms as well as guns. One kind is to bring good luck, another is to make them invisible to the animals. They rub another on the gun and think it will make their aim perfect."

"Did they teach you all that?"

"Oh yes, and more."

When they returned to the house Mama fussed over them and made them each take a dose of Venice Treacle. Patience trotted about with blankets and bowls of steaming mush. Each one made a face when his turn came for the medicine, but when they grinned at each other, Patience thought, "They're going to be friends."

She looked at Sam's fiery head.

"Why are you staring at me?" he asked. "Haven't you ever seen red hair before?"

"Is it your own?"

"Of course it's my own hair," Sam said. "Whose did you think it was? The man in the moon?"

"Your mother has a wig and it's the same colour," Patience said.

Sam laughed. "All right, I'll tell you about it. Mama's

hair all fell out when she had smallpox at Sorel, so she made Papa go into Montreal to buy her a wig. She told him to be sure to get a good bright one, because it would help to cheer her up in these dark woods. He found one the same colour as my hair and thought it a good joke on us both."

"It's as bad as being scalped," said Patience, fingering her own thick hair.

"No it isn't," said Sam. "When you've been scalped you can't wear a wig at all. A silver plate covers your brains."

Patience gasped, but she was not too horrified to continue with her questions. "Why did the Mississagys wear red coats and laced hats? Did they kill a lot of British soldiers?"

"No," Sam said indignantly. "They sold the land around Cataraqui to the government for the Loyalists, and that was part of the payment. They're very friendly."

"Will you take Miles and me out to see them?"

"I might take Miles," he said. "But there would be nary an animal or an Indian left in the woods by the time you had finished asking questions."

13

The Prophecy

Miles and Sam spent all their free time together.

"Why were you huffy before?" Miles asked one drizzly afternoon at the Tricks' as they sat eating hickory nuts and throwing the shells into the fire.

"Thought you'd be uppity because your father was a schoolmaster. What was Philadelphia like?"

"Philadelphia was a good town before the war," said Miles, "or so Mama says. I don't remember. But when the war came, Papa closed his school and went away to the army. Our friends became our enemies. They chased and taunted Patience and Honor—she's my other sister—until they had to stop going to school. I was in one fight after another but I didn't really mind. The neighbours came to hate us. Mama was always afraid they'd take our house and we'd have to go to New York, not knowing where Papa was. I'd rather have been in the army," he concluded, "with all the battles and horses and flashing swords."

"It's not like that at all," grunted Sam.

"How do you know?"

"My mother and I followed my father when he was in the army."

Miles stared at him. "I wish I could have done that!"

"You wouldn't have liked it—not unless you like bully beef, mouldy bread, and pea soup for every meal."

"There's more to life than your stomach," said Miles.

Sam flushed. "You trudge along day after day in the cold, covered with mud churned up by the wagons, doing chores whenever you make camp."

"I wouldn't care," interrupted Miles. "Just to see a battle, just once..."

"Once we were in a stinking cellar for six days. It was filled with women and children. Wounded soldiers were brought in to the floor above. We used to lie shivering and hungry on piles of dirty straw, listening to screams and groans, not knowing when we'd see Father brought in on a stretcher or if we'd see him at all ever again. Once I crept upstairs and saw an officer lying on a table. His leg was smashed and they were getting ready to cut it off. All of a sudden a cannonball came through a window and ripped off the other, then plunged through the wall."

"What happened then?"

"Luckily for him he died that night. I'll never go a-soldiering, I can tell you!"

"I will," said Miles stubbornly.

Sam lapsed into his customary silence and stared at the fire.

"What sort of a fellow was Grimble?" Miles asked.

"Big as an oak. Made my father look small. He had a wall-eye. He used to be the strongman in a country fair before he took to thievery."

"Did you ever talk to him?"

"Not me. Even the Mississagys were afraid of him and called him Crooked Eye. He could outhunt, outfish, and out-track them too. Wouldn't like to meet him alone on a trail!"

"Did you ever see his treasure hoard?" asked Miles.

"Treasure hoard?"

"My friend Trudgett told me it might still be here. Jewelled daggers, silver cups, and pieces of eight," said Miles, remembering the gory chapbooks he had secretly read into the night in Philadelphia.

"He was robbing in Canada remember, not in King George's palace."

"Did he ever come back here after he was recognized in Cataraqui?"

"No."

"Then it must still be here!" Miles lay back on the floor and toasted his feet. "I'm going to find it. See if I don't!"

"Let's find the Indians first," suggested Sam. "I haven't seen Wawatam and Musinigon for a while. We'll go tomorrow."

"If I can sneak away without Papa and Patience seeing me. He'll want me to stay and work, and she'll want to tag along."

"None of that!" said Sam.

Miles escaped successfully the next morning, and the two boys set off for the encampment. Miles was overflowing with excitement and questions.

"What are their names again? Wawatam and Musinigon—except I mustn't call them that."

"Watch out for the stump," said Sam.

Rubbing his bruised toes, Miles walked on.

"Watch that branch!"

Miles backed away from a branch that had stabbed his cheek and walked on more cautiously. Then his foot slipped and he fell into a pile of snow-covered leaves.

Sam helped him up and brushed off the wet leaves and pine-needles that clung to his clothes. "If you don't watch where you're going, you won't even reach the encampment."

"How can you talk to them?" Miles asked after he had spent ten minutes silently concentrating on where he was going.

"My uncle Hamish taught me. He was a fur-trader and he learned their language. That's what I'm going to be," he added.

He watched Miles' uncertain progress with a critical eye. "You'll have to learn to travel faster than that," he said. "Wawatam can walk sixty miles in a day and once Musinigon walked eighty to fetch a famous medicine man to cure his sick baby."

"In the snow?" snarled Miles.

"No," Sam admitted.

"Tell me about their medicine men," said Miles, whose appetite for magic had been kindled by Mrs Trick's stories.

"There are four kinds. You'd like the Jessakids best, though. If they have an enemy, no matter how far distant he is, they can make him become paralysed or palsied or covered in warts, and only a stronger medicine man can cure him."

"Will they teach me that too?" cried Miles, thinking of what he might do to Captain Castlevane.

"No."

They walked in silence. "Sam's about as frisky as a bowl of porridge this morning," Miles thought. But he forgot his irritation as a thread of pain, a mere whisper, almost a tickle, stole through a back tooth. He pretended not to feel it and licked the tooth tenderly, but the pain sliced through it again. Desperately he tried to think of something else, to concentrate on the trail, but the needle-sharp pain darted through his tooth again. Despite himself he moaned aloud.

"What's the matter now?"

"Toothache." Miles plastered snow on his jaw. "Does your mother know a cure?"

Sam looked sympathetically at his grimacing friend. "I don't think she does, but we're going to the right place for help. Old Musinigon might. Hurry, we're nearly there."

Miles barely looked at the little group of round wigwams clustered in a hollow. Sam took him into one of the wigwams and began talking to a dignified Indian with strange markings on his face and body. "That must be Musinigon," Miles thought between jabs of pain. There was also a woman and a chubby baby who was rolling about amidst yelping dogs. A young Indian with a painted face sat by the entrance.

Musinigon was smoking a pipe, and the combination of the pipe smoke, the toothache, and the dark murky wigwam made Miles suddenly long for the neat flower-scented streets of Philadelphia.

Nodding his head gravely, Musinigon left Sam and went over to the young Indian. He gestured to him with his hands. "What did he say?" Miles asked Sam. "Is he making magic already?"

"You'll see," said Sam. "He knows how to cure toothache."

"Spells and magic?"

"You'll see."

The pain came again and Miles forgot everything and collapsed on a pile of skins.

In a few moments the young Indian returned and handed Musinigon something dark that wriggled. Miles cowered among the skins. Musinigon approached slowly, his eyes gleaming above the chalky circles on his cheeks.

"What is it?"

"Don't worry," said Sam. "It's only a frog."

He listened carefully while Musinigon seemed to explain something. "You're to open your mouth," Sam said. "Hold the frog over the tooth that hurts and let the frog breathe on it. Then—"

"I'd rather have a toothache!" But Miles was ashamed to fuss before Sam and the watchful Mississagys, so he took the wriggling frog and held it up to his mouth. Terrified, it tried to escape, and Miles nearly let it slip out of his hand. Sam muttered some words of encouragement and Miles opened his mouth again. He was sure that the frog would squirm loose and jump down his throat. Finally he managed to keep the frog's mouth open over the aching tooth. He hoped it would breathe properly. There was a hush in the tent and the Mississagys stared intently. Slowly the pain ebbed away and finally it disappeared altogether.

"It's gone!" With a sigh of relief he handed the frog to Sam. The silent lodge came to life again. The baby squealed, the dogs yelped, and Sam and Musinigon talked excitedly by the fire with another Indian who had come in.

"We're in luck," said Sam. He came back to Miles and sat on the pile of skins, sniffing the reeking air delightedly. "A powerful Mida is going to visit the encampment." He pointed to the grave Indian who was talking to Musinigon (Miles thought he remembered him picking up the clock). "Wawatam says they plan to consult the Great Turtle tonight. So we're all going to the sweating-house first."

"Who's the Great Turtle?"

"One of their gods," answered Sam.

"What's a sweating-house?" asked Miles warily.

"It's to clear your head. You'll see. If you survive, 'twill make you feel better. Take off your clothes!"

"I won't! Why?"

"Do as I say," said Sam impatiently. "If you seem afraid they'll nickname you Craven Heart or Coyote. They always give every stranger a name that suits him, for good or ill."

"What's yours?" asked Miles, holding on to his clothes defiantly.

"Red Fox. Now hurry!"

Furtively Miles stripped and to his relief no one paid any attention. Naked and shivering, he ran with Sam across the clearing to a large round hut made from bent willows tightly covered with skins. They were followed by Musinigon and Wawatam who, seemingly unaffected by the cold, saw no need to run.

Musinigon carried a bark dish of water in his hand. When they entered the hut Miles saw a pile of stones in the middle. Sam had told him that the Indians often worshipped oddly shaped objects as gods, and he wondered what Mama would say if he took part in some strange pagan ceremony. He reached out to touch one of the stones but Sam pulled him back. Leaning over to Musinigon's dish, he dipped his fingers in the water and splashed the stone. The water hissed and turned to steam immediately.

"Sit down over here," said Sam.

Musinigon sprinkled more water on the stones with a cedar branch and hot waves of steam passed over them. Choking and dripping with sweat, Miles cried: "Is this an Indian torture?"

"You'll learn to like it," said Sam. By now his red hair coiled damply around his head and great beads of perspiration ran down his cheeks. "Hold your breath and shut your eyes when Musinigon throws the water on, then the steam doesn't choke you." He handed Miles a wet cedar branch. "Here," he said, "breathe through this when the steam comes."

"It's like being burned alive," groaned Miles and Musinigon threw more water on the stones. Gradually Miles became accustomed to this ritual; he no longer felt like a roasted rabbit and even began to enjoy himself. Wawatam and Musinigon talked and laughed, their bronze skins glistening with the steam. Miles noticed that Sam looked like a lobster and then saw that he did too. He thought he saw another pinkish figure through the steam but couldn't be sure.

After half an hour he found it difficult to breathe and wondered if he was suffocating.

"Come on!" yelled Sam. He grabbed Miles by the hand and raced to the entrance. He tugged Miles outside and pushed him into a pile of snow. Miles yelled, but the snow felt wonderful—not at all cold—and he rolled around in it like a puppy.

"Now for the lodge," said Sam. "Race you." They ran back to the wigwam. As Miles pulled on his clothes he thought he had never felt so exhausted yet so exhilarated in all his life. Every bone and muscle cried for sleep but his skin tingled from head to toe. He collapsed on the furs with a tremendous yawn.

"Where are the others?" he said to Sam, who had slumped beside him.

"They stay in a long time. When they come out we'll eat."

"I'm too tired to open my mouth or chew."

"You won't be," said Sam with the air of one who had survived many a sweating-house. "But sleep until they come."

"Did you notice how red we both got?" Miles said drowsily.

"I always get red in the sweating-house. We're not Indians."

"I know. But I saw someone else there who was red."

There was no reply. Sam had fallen asleep.

Roused by Wawatam and Musinigon, Miles felt ready to eat anything. He was pleased to see that Mrs Musinigon (as he called her to himself, for he was tired of asking Sam questions) was already ladling a delicious-smelling stew into clay bowls.

He looked around for the pink Indian but couldn't see him. Sam was talking eagerly to Wawatam. They looked at Miles, then laughed.

"What are they saying?" asked Miles, attempting to rise from his furry bed. He was so exhausted, it took two tries. He looked hungrily at the stew and wished that Mrs Musinigon would hurry.

"They've given you a name."

"What is it?" demanded Miles.

"Pikonekwe."

"What does it mean?"

"Little frog."

Miles winced. "Pikonekwe. Well, it doesn't sound so bad in Indian."

He stepped forward across the pile of skins to have a closer look at the stew.

"Ow! Watch where you're treadin' with your clumsy feet!" The pile erupted to produce Miles' pink Indian.

"Alf Brown!"

"Right, lad," said Alf, scrambling up. "Slow to recognize an old friend, ain't you?"

"You were all covered in dirt," explained Miles.

"No cause to wash," said Alf. "How's your family?"

"They're all fine. What are you doing here, you old robber? Why aren't you at the fort or off saving the country from its enemies?"

Sam interrupted by passing Mrs Musinigon's stew, which turned out to be a savoury dish of venison, squirrel, fish, beans, and corn.

"How is that rat Castlevane? I didn't think you'd last long in the army. Did Finlay throw you out for misbehaviour?"

"He wouldn't dare," said Alf. He spooned the stew rapidly into his mouth with his fingers. "He talks a lot, don't he?" he said to Sam.

"How did you find the Mississagys?"

"They was in Cataraqui one day, trading furs for blankets. So I took a bit o' leave, and I came back with 'em to learn their drum songs and war dances. But they're back'ard musically, very back'ard. I've been a-teaching them and they're coming on. They do seem to 'ave a knack for it."

"How do you talk to them?"

"Him as plays a drum can talk to the world," said Alf grandly.

"Are you going to 'borrow' things from the Indians too?" asked Miles as Alf carefully fished out a bulging knapsack from a flap-like pocket in the wall of the tent.

"Never!" said Alf piously. He added in a whisper: "I've

no mind to be wrapped in birchbark and set alight—that there sweating-house is hot enough for me. But I gets itchy feet, and then it's time to wander on. I'll come to see you first, though. I knows where you live. Musinigon showed me. How's your Papa? Keeping well? Life in the woods suits him, does it?''

"Well enough," said Miles. "What's in the knapsack? Who *have* you been borrowing things from? Cataraqui's not a battlefield."

Alf looked wounded. "Musinigon gave me a rattle—a shishikoi. You needn't look sneery. 'Tain't a toy but a musical instrument. There's other odds and ends in there too. Some of 'em Finlay's," he added with a grin.

"Come along, you tonguey pair," said Sam. "It's time to visit the Great Turtle."

Darkness had come. An owl hooted over their heads as they stepped out from the stuffy smoky warmth of the tent into the cold air. Indians came from the other lodges and they walked along together to another wigwam.

Everyone crowded inside. Miles looked around by the light of the fires and saw that in the middle of the floor there had been placed another smaller wigwam made of mooseskins drawn over a wooden framework.

"That's for the medicine man and the Great Turtle," said Sam in a low voice.

Miles was awed by the flames that transformed the dark figures into eerie creatures from another world. "You seem to know a lot about this."

"Uncle Hamish became a Wabeno—that's a medicine man," said Sam.

The mooseskins had been lifted up and the medicine man, nearly naked, crept into the small tent on his hands and knees. Even before he disappeared inside, the small wigwam began to shake and barks and howls sounded from within. They were joined by human voices. The Indians hissed these voices angrily.

Then there was utter silence until, from inside the tent, there came a faint voice like the cry of a very young puppy. The Indians began clapping their hands.

"What are they saying?" asked Miles.

"The Great Turtle, 'the Spirit that never lies,' has come," said Sam, who was clapping as joyously as the rest.

They heard songs from inside the wigwam; then the medicine man spoke hoarsely and said that the Great Turtle had come and would answer questions.

Wawatam put several handfuls of tobacco into the tent. He spoke to the Great Spirit rapidly and anxiously.

"He's making a tobacco offering," said Sam. "The Indians always make them to their gods."

"What is he saying?"

"Wawatam wants to know if he and his brothers can trust the British."

The Spirit spoke and the medicine man repeated his answers in Ojibwa.

Sam translated for Miles. "He says that the British will fill their canoes with presents, with blankets, kettles, guns, and large barrels of rum such as the stoutest of Indians will not be able to lift."

Then the other Indians made offerings of tobacco and asked their questions.

Miles saw everyone else receiving answers that pleased them; he felt that he would like to pose a question too. He tugged at Sam's sleeve. "Will you ask one for me?"

"But you have no offering."

"Take some o' mine," offered Alf, who had been sitting

quietly beside them. "Here." He dug and wriggled around in his clothes until he triumphantly uncovered a small pouch. "It's the very best kinni-kinnic," he said.

"Ask the Great Turtle if my sister Honor is safe and if we will ever see her again." Nervously he crept forward with Sam and thrust Alf's tobacco into the inner wigwam. He did not believe in the Spirit, but felt oddly anxious as Sam asked the question.

The tent shuddered violently; the Spirit gave a great cry and there was utter silence. Miles sat mute and bewildered. Had the Spirit been angered by a question from an impudent Bostonese? Had Alf's tobacco not been acceptable, or had he driven the Great Turtle away with his question? But the Indians sat quietly and patiently, so he waited too.

The tent shuddered as if a wind had entered, and the medicine man announced that the Spirit had come again. It delivered a harangue. Sam listened intently and translated for Miles.

"Your sister will return as surely as trees walk, liars tell the truth, and there is honour among thieves."

"What does it mean? That she *won't* return? Where is she?" Miles was baffled. Alf obligingly emptied his pouch of tobacco for another offering; but despite Sam's entreaties, no sound came from the Spirit.

The medicine man came out of the tent, pale and exhausted, with the message that the Great Turtle had left.

"Do you believe in his prophecies?" Miles asked Sam as the three of them walked through the moonlight.

"Yes...no. I don't know." Sam yawned.

"I always believe the cheerful ones," said Alf.

"Well, I'm for bed," Sam said when they had returned to

the friendly warmth of Musinigon's wigwam. He flung himself down on the furs with a happy sigh.

"What a day this has been," Miles said, feeling his tooth. He put away the thought of what Papa would say about staying away all night, deciding to worry about that tomorrow.

Before dawn the next morning Miles and Sam said goodbye to Alf and the Indians and left the encampment. As the cold December sun rose, Miles prepared himself for Papa's inevitable wrath.

"I wonder if he will flog me," he said to Sam. "At least I can tell him what the Great Turtle said. Maybe that will distract him. What do you suppose the prophecy meant? If only I could reach Quebec or go to England to search for Honor. There's been no answer yet to Papa's letters."

He stared at the half-frozen stream that ran near the trail. Chunks of ice glinted in the sun like jewels. He stopped.

"Grimble's treasure! The very thing. Do you remember? If I find it we could begin the search—and perhaps there'd be enough left of the reward to purchase my commission."

"Dreamer!"

"Wet-blanket!"

They grinned at each other.

"You're hopeless," said Sam. "Still, I'll help you."

14

Sam's Secret

Miles could smell breakfast as he cautiously opened the door of the hut.

"Miles!" Patience spotted him first.

Mama rushed over and hugged him.

"Well, Miles," said Papa. "Did you see Musinigon?"

Miles gaped. "How—?"

"Two sets of footprints in the snow leading east in the direction of the Indian camp. One surefooted in following a trail; the other clumsy and sprawling. *That's* how I knew!" Papa smiled at Miles.

"Why did you worry me so, Miles?" Mama said. "Sit down and eat before you catch a cold."

"Don't flap about, Abby," said Papa.

"He must eat his breakfast," said Mama. "Who knows what strange concoctions he has been eating. Poor lamb."

"Your poor lamb is now a strapping thirteen and quite capable of fending for himself," said Papa. He lit his pipe and rearranged himself on his sack. "Now, tell us of your jaunt."

Miles glowed with pride.

"I've news of Honor—of a sort," he added hastily as he saw Mama's eyes blaze with hope.

"No, the Mississagys haven't seen her," he said before she questioned him, "but I asked the Great Turtle and it made a prophecy."

Patience said: "The Great Turtle? What is that?"

"It's a spirit."

"A spirit! Did you see it?"

"You don't *see* a spirit, beetle skull! I *heard* it."

"Miles! What did it say?" Mama was exasperated with this exchange. "What were you told about Honor?"

"Honor will return as surely as trees walk, liars tell the truth, and there is honour among thieves."

"And sense among the Averys," said Papa.

"James! That means Honor will never return!" Mama wailed.

"Now Abby, calm yourself. You're not to believe such rubbish!"

"What else did the spirit say?" Mama asked Miles.

"Nothing. It went away—at least that's what we were told. It wouldn't say any more."

"It had retired to enjoy its tobacco offerings," said Papa. "Was the medicine man exhausted when he crawled out from under the inner tent?"

"Yes, but how did you know?"

"I saw a similar ceremony among the tribes on the Mississippi."

"Did you visit a sweating-house too?" Miles asked eagerly.

"Yes." Papa smiled at the memory. "In fact, you and Sam must discover from your friend Musinigon how to build one. 'Tis a most invigorating custom. Now, alas, we must return to more mundane tasks." He knocked out his pipe in the fireplace, laid it on the shelf beside the clock, and picked up an axe from the corner. "Admire your sister's pet, Miles, and then we'll talk Indian customs as we chop."

"Come down to the stream with me, Abby, and show me the rocks you want moved for the dam."

"How do you like my bird?" Patience asked as she and Miles finished their breakfast. She had been waiting eagerly for him to notice a little drooping-winged jay. "I found it under the big fir tree. It has a broken wing and I'm allowed to keep it."

Miles absent-mindedly stroked its bright feathers. "What will you call it?" he asked.

"Hodge."

"That's a cat's name," he scoffed, but Patience ignored him and tried to persuade Hodge to eat the bread crumbs from breakfast.

"How would you like to hunt for treasure?" Miles asked.

"What treasure?"

"The bandit's hoard."

"You mean Grimble's?"

"Yes, and Sam's going to help us find it. Sam told me that he never came back after he was seen in Cataraqui, so it must be hidden around here."

"What did he have?" asked Patience. "Would there be emeralds and pearls and gold pieces?"

"No, silly," said Miles. "There will likely be silver watches and coins from travellers' purses. He wasn't robbing King George's palace, you know."

"When shall we start looking?"

"We'll wait for Sam. Oh, I forgot. Alf Brown's with the Indians!"

"He is? Will he come to see us?"

"Yes."

"I'm glad. But I wish there were some girls in these woods."

"There is one, with the Indians."

"How old is she?"

"Two!"

"Peck him, Hodge!"

"Miles!" called Papa, and "Patience!" called Mama, as if in a distant duet. Each went to a parent to perform the daily chores.

Sam did not appear after all. When Miles and Patience grew tired of waiting for him they devoted their spare time over the next two days to searching the house and the clearing. They found nothing. They dug in the sacks in the corner, although they knew that Mama had been all through them. They even dug in the dirt floor under the bed and rooted around inside the dried leaves in the mattress. Still they found nothing.

One morning Sam did appear.

"Why are you waddling like a duck?" Miles asked, looking with interest at Sam's ungainly footgear. "What's that on your feet?"

"Snowshoes," said Sam. "D'you want to try them?"

The snowshoes had a frame of tough wood, pointed at either end and wide in the middle. Over the frame was spread an open network of woven narrow deer-thongs. They were bound to Sam's moccasins by an intricate series of straps and loops.

Sam undid the straps and knelt down and tied the shoes on Miles' feet.

"Off you go!" he said.

Miles stood up, tried to lift one foot, and promptly fell

over backwards. "Since I met you, Sam Trick," he spluttered as he emerged from a snowdrift, "I've spent half my life buried in snow."

"Let *me* try," said Patience, but Miles shook his head and persevered until he had managed to stagger all around the clearing.

"What sport!" he puffed as he collapsed in a heap beside Sam. "Can I try them along the trail?"

"All right," said Sam agreeably. Miles tightened the straps, waved, and soon had vanished among the trees.

Sam sat whistling at Hodge. Tiring of that, he began to throw snowballs at Patience. When she threw them back he always dodged in time and missed being hit. Furious at him, at Miles, and at herself for being a girl, she picked up a stick and began tracing letters in a bank of fresh snow.

"Sam Trick is a snirp," she printed angrily on the glistening white surface, expecting a handful of wet snow down her neck at any moment. But Sam had wandered over empty-handed and was watching with interest.

"What does it say?" he asked.

"You mean you can't read?"

"No one ever taught me. My parents are but indifferent scholars and there has been little time for learning in our wanderings."

"What fun!" said Patience. " 'Twill be just like 'Giles Gingerbread.' " And for a fleeting moment she wondered if Mama could be persuaded to make all the letters of the alphabet out of gingerbread, for her and Sam to study and eat. "But we haven't any ginger and it would spoil the surprise," she said aloud.

"What surprise?" said Sam, tracing the letters curiously with his finger.

"I'll teach you how to read, and we won't tell anyone until you can. I'll show you some letters on the snow today."

Patience began by having Sam recite "a ba ca da" with her. His eagerness shamed Patience, who remembered how she had hated it when Mama tried to teach her—she had escaped her lessons at every chance. To her mortification she discovered that she had forgotten most of the verses from the primer that she had once had by heart. All she could remember was:

> *In Adam's fall*
> *We sinned all.*
>
> *Thy life to mend,*
> *God's Book attend.*
>
> *The Cat doth play,*
> *And after slay.*
>
> *A Dog will bite*
> *A thief at night.*
>
> *The idle Fool*
> *Is whipped at school.*

"There are lots more verses," she told him, "but I can't remember them."

Sam fell upon learning with the hunger of a starved wolf. Patience quietly lent him her books. He in turn lent Miles his snowshoes every day in order to get rid of him. The treasure was forgotten.

"You really love to read, don't you?" Patience asked Sam one afternoon. He had been reading aloud, scarcely stumbling except over words she herself had always skipped.

"Yes," he said, his eyes straying to the next words on the page.

"I wish I could teach you cyphering too."

Sam looked up from his book. "Can't you?"

She shook her head and recited for Sam:

> *Multiplication is my vexation,*
> *And Division quite as bad,*
> *The Golden rule is my stumbling stule,*
> *And Practice makes me mad.*

"That's no use," he said.

The same day Miles limped in, complaining of mysterious aches and pains in his legs.

"Snowshoe evil," said Sam.

"What's that?"

"It's from snowshoeing too much. You'll have to stay around here for a week or so."

"Sam, please stay for supper," Patience said excitedly. "We'll surprise them all afterwards when you read." She could hardly wait for Papa to return from his everlasting chopping. She ran to meet him as he walked wearily in from the far edge of the clearing. His face was streaked with sweat and dirt and he had wood chips in his hair. He seemed to take forever to wash himself in the clumsy wooden bowl he had hacked out of a log. Then he sank onto the bed and closed his eyes.

"Oh, Papa, don't go to sleep! I have something to tell you. Please wake up!" Papa opened his eyes and closed them again.

"I'm listening. What is it, Miss Impatience?"

Patience smiled encouragingly at Sam, who stared into the fire. Miles sat beside him groaning over his snowshoe evil.

"Papa, did you know that when we came here Sam couldn't read?"

"That *is* unfortunate! You're a sharp lad, Sam. Did you have poor schoolmasters?"

"Never had any," mumbled Sam.

"But now he can read!" Patience cried. "Listen!" She pulled *Aesop's Fables* from the shelf. Sam read a page with a flourish.

"Harder!" said Patience, handing him *Gulliver's Travels*. He read that.

"Harder still!" She pulled out John Locke's *Essays*, and not until she absent-mindedly handed him a Latin grammar did Sam stumble.

"Remarkable!" said Papa who by now was sitting up, his weariness forgotten. "How did you learn so quickly?"

"I taught him," said Patience.

"I am proud of both of you."

Miles, irritated from his sore leg, muttered: "Pooh! I could read books like that when I was nine. Reading isn't so hard."

Sam looked at him, then pulled a roll of birchbark from his pocket, wrote something quickly, and handed it to Miles. "Read this!" he said.

Miles took it confidently. Instead of words he knew, he looked at a group of strange stick-like figures. "I don't know," he admitted. "It looks like one of Patience's drawings."

Sam took it back and read: "The hunter who can read only his own tracks will catch a fool."

Miles grinned. "Give it to me," he said. "I, Pikonekwe, will hang it on the wall."

"What's all this?" asked Papa. "Indian writing?"

Patience interrupted. "Papa, you said you would start to teach us as soon as we were snowed in. Can you start now and can Sam come?"

"It will be a pleasure to teach such an eager scholar," said Papa with a grin. And so it was settled.

The Evening School flourished. Miles worked hard, determined not to be outdone by Sam, who gave himself wholly to every task Papa set him.

At first Sam came alone, but one bitter night, when he arrived shaking snowflakes from his cap and rubbing his ears, he was followed by Mr Trick, who grinned sheepishly and said: "The boy talks of nothing all day but school and books. Maggie said: 'It would do you no harm, you great lump, to learn something besides crops and soldiering,' so here I am."

Papa was delighted to have an extra pupil, and Mr Trick always came after that. As Sam rattled off his lessons, he would beam with pride.

They spent many cheerful evenings by the blazing fire that lit the hut. No matter how tired and discouraged Papa was after a day of wrestling with logs, he revived when he began to teach, and roared enthusiastically at child and neighbour alike. Fortunately Mr Trick was a good-humoured man. He took it calmly when Papa called him "Booby" or "Mutton-head!" At times he dozed off comfortably by the fire, though he always managed to be awake when it was his turn to read.

Once lessons were over Papa would play a wooden flute that he had carved, while the children cracked nuts and roasted small pumpkins in the shell. Often Mrs Trick came along too. Although she refused to take part in the lessons, she listened approvingly as the others read aloud. Miles begged her for more ghost stories but there was never enough time.

"Perhaps Christmas night," she promised. "We'll spend it together, shall we? I like to celebrate Hogmanay myself, but Simon and Sammy, they're great ones for Christmas."

15

Christmas Day

"O Dormouse, sleepy dormouse, Venture from your blanket house." Miles laid an icy hand on Patience's cheek.

"You'd *better* be an officer," she yawned, trying to bury her head under the blanket. "You'll never be a poet."

"Get dressed! Have you forgotten? It's Christmas. The Tricks are coming for dinner and Mama wants decorations." Miles had already gathered an armload of bittersweet and handed her a spray of the bright red berries. "We'll need more of these and pine boughs and cones too."

Patience scrambled hastily into her dress. Papa called it her frock of many colours, for Mama had sewn every imaginable kind of fur upon it: squirrel, rabbit, deer, muskrat, and beaver. Patience loved it dearly and felt like an Indian princess whenever she wore it. Miles said she was such a prickly character it should be made of porcupine quills, but she had learned to ignore his teasing—most of the time.

As Mama gave her breakfast Patience saw that a kettle of pea soup was already simmering on the fire; there were two loaves of bread growing brown and crusty in the ashes. Mama had paid close attention to her baking lessons with Mrs Trick.

Miles and Patience worked all morning, attended by Hodge, who nearly got stepped on several times. Mama made a large evergreen wreath and Papa dragged in a yule log. He sniffed the air appreciatively. "Pea soup, pine boughs, and freshly baked bread. I would not exchange such fragrances for all the perfumes of Araby. When do the Tricks arrive?"

Branches festooned the walls and twined around the stump-table. The bittersweet berries glowed on the shelf, in the centre of the table, and even on top of the clock. Patience had made a collar of berries for an indignant Hodge. She spent the last hour going to the door and looking out hopefully for the Tricks. "They'll never come," she said.

"Perhaps a bear—" Miles was interrupted by voices singing outside.

> *Wassail, wassail, out of the milk pail,*
> *Wassail, wassail, as white as my nail,*
> *Wassail, wassail, in snow, frost and hail,*
> *Wassail, wassail, with partridge and rail,*
> *Wassail, wassail, that much doth avail,*
> *Wassail, wassail, that never will fail.*

Papa opened the door and there stood all the Tricks beaming.

"I always say, Christmas dinner is a time to cram and stuff as much as you like," said Mrs Trick, handing Mama a venison pie, an enormous bilberry currant tart, and a bottle of red currant wine. Sam and Mr Trick followed her in, their arms laden with baskets of provisions.

They began their celebration with a Christmas service. Sam read the lesson while his parents gazed admiringly. They sang "While shepherds watched their flocks by night," and Mama sang the "Cherry tree Carol," which had been Honor's favourite.

Later they sat down to a dinner that satisfied even Mrs Trick with the number and variety of its dishes. There was wild roast turkey with cranberry jelly, wild pigeons and fish, venison pie, honey and squash, and pumpkin bread. Then they had Mrs Trick's tart for dessert. They ate and talked happily while Mama and Mrs Trick kept refilling the wooden bowls and mugs.

"A feast fit for a bashaw with nine tails, eh, my bald-headed eaglet?" said Mr Trick to his wife. He took out a horn snuffbox and offered Papa a pinch.

"Snuff won't be common here yet awhile," he said, and he sneezed so violently that his eyebrows flew up and down. "So I keep it for special occasions. What it lacks in style it makes up in strength."

At that moment he caught sight of Hodge, who was pecking crumbs from the floor.

"What's that bird doing here?" he asked.

"It's my blue jay," Patience told him.

Mr Trick looked at Hodge with disapproval. "I don't hold with birds, except in pies," he said, "ever since I was a little boy in England and had to act as a crowherd to keep the pests out of the garden." In a high falsetto voice he piped:

> *Away, away, away birds;*
> *Take a little bit and come another day, birds;*
> *Great birds, little birds, pigeons and crows,*
> *I'll up with my clackers and down she goes.*

While the adults sampled Mr Trick's wine, Patience, Sam, and Miles roasted nuts and told riddles by the fire.

"You first, Sam," said Miles, popping a hot nut into his mouth and hastily spitting it out again as it burnt his tongue. Sam thought for a moment.

> *Highty-tighty, paradighty,*
> *Clothed all in green,*
> *The king could not read it,*
> *No more could the queen;*
> *They sent for the wise man*
> *From out of the East,*
> *Who said it had horns,*
> *But was not a beast.*

"Who doesn't know that?" Patience said. "It's a holly."

"Well, you say one," said Sam.

> *In marble walls as white as milk,*
> *Lined with a skin as soft as silk,*
> *Within a fountain crystal-clear,*
> *A golden apple doth appear.*
> *No doors there are to this stronghold,*
> *Yet thieves break in and steal the gold.*

Miles groaned loudly. "An egg."

"You tell one since you're so smart," said Sam.

Miles thought for a moment.

> *He went to the wood and caught it,*
> *He sat him down and sought it;*
> *Because he could not find it,*
> *Home with him he brought it.*

Silence.

"I give up," said Sam.

"I do too," said Patience.

"It's a sliver."

"Now for some Christmas pie, my nutcrackers," said Mr Trick with a twinkle from beneath his eyebrows, and Sam produced a huge pie from the bag in which Mrs Trick had brought her share of the provisions.

"We are in danger of being over-venisoned and over-pigeoned," protested Papa, belching comfortably. Sam handed Patience his jackknife with a flourish, and she plunged it eagerly into the crust. What would appear? Plums, berries, or some of Mrs Trick's precious apples, brought from Cataraqui and hoarded during the winter?

"Four-and-twenty blackbirds baked in a pie," sang Mr Trick, glancing at Hodge.

The knife cut through air. "You're joking me," Patience said. "There's nothing in it."

"Hidden treasure!" Sam whispered.

"Come now, don't tease," said Mrs Trick. "Lift off the crust, Sammy."

Sam did so and revealed a pie full of presents. For Mama there was a cherry rolling-pin. It was extra long and the red-brown wood had been polished to a satiny-smooth finish.

"What huge pies I shall make with this," said Mama. "Pies to satisfy the appetite of a Grimble!"

For Miles there was a deerskin sheath filled with arrows. The birchbark case for pens could only have been meant for Papa. And nestled at the bottom of the pie there was a soft warm squirrel-skin bonnet. Despite the heat and stuffiness of the crowded room, Patience put it on at once and sat blissfully roasting.

"How very kind," began Mama, "but—"

"Pish, tush," said Mrs Trick briskly. " 'Tis but a token of gratitude for teaching our Sammy to be a scholar."

"Samuel and Miles must persevere with their lessons," said Papa seriously. "They are both clever cubs and this country will need men of education as well as farmers to guide her destiny."

Everyone looked sober at the thought of Miles and Sam guiding the country, while Patience felt hurt that she was not included in this imposing future.

"But I'm forgetting that Miles will become a general in His Majesty's army," added Papa. "Such a waste of a good education."

"I'll write you long letters about my glorious campaigns," replied Miles.

"The English army..." said Mrs Trick. "Whippings and press-gangs too. They're black-hearted ingrates, that's what they are."

"Now, Mag. Calm yourself," said Mr Trick.

"How can you be so tame, Simon? Trick by name and tricked by the army, that's you!"

"What happened?" asked Miles, scenting a story.

"Tell 'em how you was bamboozled into the army," said Mrs Trick indignantly.

"How I *joined* the army?" said Mr Trick. He winked at Miles and Sam. "Well, 'twas all a mistake, but I gained my greatest treasure from it—and that's you, my fierce canary. My poor parents died of the putrid fever when I was just a tad. Cast upon the parish, I was, and lucky not to be sent to the poor's house. But the vicar kept me to run messages and to sing in the choir, for I had a sweet voice in those far-off days.

"I was sent to the market-town one summer's day, and I went all agog to see the goings-on, for St Elfrith's-by-the-

Wold was a small village and the town seemed a metropolis of mobs to me, with people and cattle and sheep and pigs and chickens all halloing and hollering at once. The old vicar had given me a coin to buy a meal in a tavern, and I was a-sitting by the window enjoying the crowds and my meat-pasty when up strides a soldier. He sits down beside me, claps me on the back, calls me a fine fellow, and hands me a mug of beer. I'd had beer once before at haying time and liked it well enough then, so I swallowed it down, for the town was hot and dusty to my country throat.

"'Done!' he bellows, 'Come along o' me, for you've enlisted in His Majesty's army.'

"'I've not!'

"'Oh yes you have,' he said, tugging me by the arm. 'Look 'ee there.' And sure enough, at the bottom of my mug I saw fat George's pence. I'd taken the king's shilling. So off to the wars I went, and fought all over North America, too, I did.''

"Murdering Sassenachs!'' muttered Mrs Trick.

"But it all turned out well enough,'' said Mr Trick cheerfully. "I never took much to soldiering, but I met Maggie, and I'd never have done *that* in St Elfrith's-by-the-Wold. Now I have a farm of my own, even if it *is* covered in trees, and that too would never have come about in England. Sammy's happy in the woods, and my old trout here can warble ditties about Prince Charlie to her heart's content. Can't you, my frizzle-frizz top?'' He tugged affectionately at Mrs Trick's ear. "Come Mag, let's sing 'How Stands the Glass Around' for the folks. 'Twas General Wolfe's favourite and it's mine too.'' And he and Mrs Trick clasped hands and sang.

"Now everyone go skating except me,'' he said at the end of the song. "I want my forty winks.''

Mama and Mrs Trick declined, but the rest erupted noisily into the clearing with new skates of bone and deer-sinews that Miles and Sam had made. They raced down to the creek, which Papa had finished damming a week before to make a small pond. It was now frozen.

The air was cold. Their noses turned red and their breath came out in little smoky puffs. The stark black and white of trees and snow was warmed by the yellow branches of the willows that seemed to have captured and held the winter sunlight.

Papa tied on Patience's skates. "Stay away from the dam," he called to Miles. "The ice may be thin there."

Sam stumbled and lurched across the pond, finally stopping by hurtling into a snowbank on the other side. Miles managed to stand up, but he couldn't move. "Give me a push, Patience," he said.

Patience skated behind him and started to shove. She pushed him across the pond faster and faster, and Sam looked up after struggling out of the snowbank to see Miles careening towards him, waving his arms and yelling "Gangway!" There was a great crash and they both disappeared in a white cloud. They dragged themselves out of the snowbank and chased Patience around the pond, shouting threats after her as she skated out of reach. Papa sat on a log and watched the whirling chase. The boys charged madly from snowbank to snowbank, unable to turn, while Patience dodged between them. Finally they cornered her near the dam.

"Ready, Sam?" called Miles.

"Ready."

"Charge!" They rushed at her. Patience waited until the last minute and then ducked under their arms and skated along the ice. Miles and Sam crashed together, and with a rending groan the ice gave way. They dropped into three feet of icy water.

"You *are* a bird-witted pair," said Papa as he held out a long branch and they pulled themselves out. "Back to the house with you. Patience, run ahead and tell Mama to prepare warm blankets and to dig out the Venice Treacle again."

"I never saw such lads for scrapes," said Mrs Trick when the boys dripped and shivered into the house.

"Venice Treacle for Miles and Sam," Patience called cheerfully, bringing Mama's bag.

They both made faces as they swallowed their medicine.

"And one for you too, Miss Patience," said Papa.

"But Papa! I didn't fall in the water!"

"Call it rough justice."

The boys huddled by the fire. Then Mr Trick, who seemed to have been slumbering all through the bustle, suddenly burst forth with:

> *Nose, nose, jolly red nose,*
> *What gave thee thy jolly red nose?*
> *Nutmeg and cinnamon, ginger and cloves,*
> *That's what gave me my jolly red nose.*

The wolves were howling in the distance when the Tricks began to say good night and put on their cloaks and coats to go home.

"Perhaps you should pass the night here," said Mama, trying to think where she would put everyone. Mr Trick picked up a thick stick that he had left by the door and twirled it menacingly.

"No wolf need think that it will befrighten *me* with the sight of it," he said. "Bless you all. Good night."

16

Miles Digs

During the winter Miles made snowshoes for all the Averys. Patience wove countless willow baskets for storing things; she also made brooms from cedar branches tied with strips of deerskin, and reread all her own books four times and Papa's twice. Papa made chairs and put up more shelves, and every corner of the house was filled with their activities. Miles whittled a flute and carved a chess set. At night they sang and argued about the best way to trap beaver, or Papa talked about the government their new country should have. The family Bible provided an endless supply of stories, lessons, and discussions.

They never ceased to wonder at the way the snow transformed the bleak and gloomy forest.

"It glitters like fairyland, or Cinderella's cloak," Patience would say as she admired the pine trees that sparkled with patches of fresh snow on their branches like jewelled buckles. The snow lay in deep heaps on the ground as if flung down by a careless giant.

After every snowstorm they had to tunnel a path to the creek. Miles and Patience spent hours building forts, walls, and snowmen. "I hope the snow never goes away," Miles would say as they came in for supper. But as the snow fell remorselessly from leaden skies well into March, he changed his mind.

They discovered that Grimble had built hastily but not well. The chinking began to fall out from between the logs and they had to dig beneath the snow in a painful search for moss to repair it. The water in the kettle was frozen every morning, and they grew accustomed to finding snow on their pillows when they woke up. In order to stay warm at night, they wore all their clothes to bed.

Mama began to look anxious as she saw their rapidly dwindling supply of flour and pork, and she worried aloud about the danger of scurvy because of the lack of fresh vegetables. She cut the meals down to two a day; one of them was gruel and dried pumpkin.

"Your father says his powder supply is low," she said to Patience, "and he must conserve it for emergencies."

"I'll set some snares," offered Miles.

"You're not to leave the clearing," Mama said sharply. "Before your father went for wood he warned me that a blizzard is brewing. I only hope that he finds his way home safely from these miserable woods."

Winter slackened its hold upon the woods early in April. The snow began to melt.

"It's clear today," Miles said to Patience, sniffing the damp air. "I'm not coming in until I find Grimble's treasure. I'm going to search every nook and cranny of this place. Tell Mama I'm building a fort if she wonders what I'm doing."

All through the long dripping morning Miles dug near trees and burrowed like a mole into snowbanks. He tried to think where he would bury his loot if he were a robber, but with a whole forest to explore, one spot seemed as good as another. His feet became numb and his hands tingled painfully and turned blue, but he dug on.

Late in the afternoon Patience came out. "Mama says you are to stop flitting about the clearing like a clunch and come in at once."

At dinner the hut seemed too hot and he pushed his supper away untouched.

"You're a rude fellow," said Papa, but Mama looked at him closely.

"The silly lumpkin has taken a cold, rooting about in the slush all day," she said. She gave him one of Mrs Trick's nasty root-and-berry mixtures for colds and fevers and made him go to bed.

"I can't be sick now," Miles thought desperately. "Keep hunting for the treasure," he said to Patience. "Get Sam to help you."

For the next few days Miles was never quite sure whether he was awake or dreaming. He felt as if warm mud were oozing up and down inside his legs and arms, weighing him down in the bed with its hot heaviness. He dreamt that Malachi Grimble had come for his treasure. He was ten feet high with a black patch over one eye, and the woods shook as he approached.

After several days of misery, Miles woke up feeling cool. The door was open and sunlight shone into the room. He could hear the trickling of water. Mama and Mrs Trick were talking quietly by the fire.

"Once the fever breaks," Mrs Trick said cheerfully,

"he'll wake up fit enough, although he'll be as thin as a wafer from not eating all these days."

"Now that Miles is getting better and spring has come," said Mama, "I can almost reconcile myself to this harsh life—"

"Gammon!" said Mrs Trick. "It won't be harsh for long. I am a farmer's wife and a farmer's daughter and I know good land when I see it. Soon we shall all live as high as coach-horses. Why, Simon has promised to build me a fine stone house within five years, and," she patted her wig reflectively, "I shall keep peacocks!"

This announcement was acknowledged from the bed. "Peacocks!"

Mama and Mrs Trick jumped up. Mrs Trick's rosy face grew even rosier. "Peacocks," she said firmly, and felt Miles' forehead.

"I thought so," she said. "Cool as a custard. What would you say, sir, to some soup and a piece of bread and honey?"

"Yes, please," said Miles hungrily. "Where's Patience?"

Mrs Trick laughed. "She and Sammy have grown very thick since your illness. Now the snow's melted and it's easier to get back and forth, they've been scurrying around the place together from dawn to dusk for days."

"Look what we found!"

In ran Patience, clutching a small furry ball. Sam followed her with another.

"What is it?" said Miles.

"Fox cubs." Sam laid his red bundle on the bed.

"Their mother is dead," said Patience, "and these two poor little things were yapping like terriers all by themselves in the woods. Can we keep them, Mama? I want to call mine Barnaby. They'll be company for Hodge."

"They'll probably eat him," Mama said. But she went to the stump-table to find some scraps.

"This is the only treasure we found," Patience whispered to Miles. "We looked everywhere. Grimble must have taken it with him. Or perhaps he spent it all before he ever got here."

That night, as Miles lay with Reynard, his fox cub, curled at his feet, he heard Papa talking by the fire.

"Now that the weather is breaking, the river will open and there may be some word of Honor. I should go to Cataraqui to find out. And to settle our score with Castlevane and get clear title to our land."

"It would all be so much easier if we were not as poor as church mice and forced to count every penny," said Mama. "Then you could go to Quebec."

"I *must* find the treasure," Miles thought, "and then we'd get the reward."

Mama made him stay in bed next morning. "In bed you stay, my boy, until you are recovered!" she said firmly.

Patience took Hodge outside while Mama cleaned the house. "It's a pigpen," she said, looking severely at Barnaby and Reynard. "Or rather it's a menagerie."

The morning dragged on. Miles turned over restlessly in the big bed. Papa was checking his traps and Mama and Patience had gone hunting for firewood. Papa had suggested that he do some Latin grammar, but Miles did not feel like studying. He tossed the book over onto the table, but it hit the side of the stump, bounced off, and skidded over the dirt floor.

Papa hotly disapproved of mistreating books. Miles, thinking of the bad mood Papa had been in when he had left in the morning, crawled out of bed to retrieve it. He tripped over one of the roots of the stump-table where the dirt had been brushed away. "We're always tripping over that pesky root," he thought. "I'll cut it off."

He pulled out his knife and began to hack away at the root. It was as tough as the stump itself and he began to despair of removing it. He managed to cut a notch in the root where it joined the stump. He tried to dig the earth away from the root in order to get hold of it and break it off the stump. The dirt floor was packed hard but he loosened the root with his knife and began to scoop earth away from underneath. The root ended abruptly after about ten inches. He cleaned away the earth and sat back to contemplate ways of breaking it off. The root was about as thick as his wrist and projected from the stump down into the hole he had dug in the floor.

Miles knelt down and gripped the root with both hands. He pulled to try to snap it off. Nothing happened. He went over to the door and brought back the strong stick that he usually carried when he went out into the woods. "This should do the trick," he thought. "I'll wedge it under the root and lever it up." He stuck the stick into the hole and heaved. Instead of breaking the root as he expected, the whole stump moved.

It wasn't growing there at all. He gave it another heave and was interrupted by Mama, carrying a bundle of twigs.

"Miles! Why are you out of bed? And you just over a fever. What fools my children are." She propelled Miles back to bed.

Miles was in an agony of excitement to tell Patience. "Fetch Sam!" he said when she gave him his dinner. "We have to move the tree stump."

She stared at him. "What tree stump?"

"The table, you booby. I can't move it all by myself. We'll need Sam."

She gazed at the stump absent-mindedly, her mind on Barnaby, who was frisking about the room chasing his tail. "Why shouldn't it stay where it is? It seems a good place."

"Doughhead! We must move it to see what's underneath. I think Grimble hid the treasure there!"

"Oh!" Patience ran for her cloak and said to Mama: "You wanted to give Mrs Trick the herb seedlings. Can I take them over for you?"

"Won't you be afraid?" said Mama doubtfully. "I never knew you to relish a long lonely walk before, Patience."

"Please let me. I'll bring Sam back with me to entertain Miles."

"Our Patience is becoming a tiger," Mama said rather wistfully to Miles. "Very well," she told Patience, "but I think I'll come too."

"Don't let me find you rooting about on the floor when I get back," she told Miles as she put on her shawl. "You may put another log on the fire, but then you must hop back into bed immediately."

They closed the door and Miles lay back and dreamed of the treasure.

17

Soot and Snuff

At last the door opened and Patience and Sam puffed in.
"Mama stayed for a chat with Mrs Trick," Patience said.
"We ran as fast as we could."

"Patience says you've struck treasure," said Sam. "I'm
surprised you aren't counting it already."

"I haven't found anything yet—except a hole," said
Miles jumping out of bed. "Look, dig all the dirt away from
the bottom of the stump around the roots." When Sam did
this, Miles said: "Now we'll need your rope." Sam unwound
the Indian rope he always wore around his waist. "Tie it
around the root and you and Patience pull while I lever it
up."

"One, two, three, pull!" The stump lifted and moved
forward a little. Inch by inch they jerked it across the floor.

"Making a tree walk is hard work," said Patience.

Sam and Miles stared at her. "You're right, Patience. It's
a good omen," Miles said. "Let's keep on."

Slowly as the mighty stump moved toward them, a hole
appeared in the floor.

The three of them looked at each other and then, almost afraid of what they might see, peered inside.

A small wooden box bound in brass sat there. Miles tried to lift it out, but it was too heavy. He pried the top up with his jackknife, first in one place, then in another and another. It had been well secured. Finally, enough of it was free for Miles and Sam to lift it clear of the box.

"We're rich!" shrieked Patience.

Gold and silver watches, coins, and jewels gleamed in the darkness.

"I knew it was there!" cried Miles.

Sam looked at the treasure quietly. "You know what this means, don't you? He'll be back!"

They stared at each other uneasily and looked around the hut for shelter, as if Grimble had suddenly appeared in the doorway.

"What can we do?" Patience asked timidly.

Sam scratched his head and watched the dancing flames of the fire. Then he laughed aloud.

"I have it! We'll prepare a surprise for him. But we'll have to work quickly. Now that the ice has broken, Grimble will be able to come and go easily by canoe. If we are lucky the Mississagys will be able to warn us when he comes around here. I saw Musinigon yesterday. I'll ask him to send me any word he hears of Grimble. This is what we'll do if he comes . . ."

Miles and Patience looked at him admiringly after he had described his plan.

"How did you think of it?" asked Patience.

"Read it in one of your books."

"It's capital," said Miles. "Now pull the stump back and cover up the treasure. We won't tell Mama and Papa yet. We'll surprise them."

Papa had a surprise of his own when he came in, accompanied by Mr Trick.

"Hello, Sam," he said. "Your father has found tracks about. We're going after deer."

"Where are they?" Sam asked.

"Just along the trail," said his father.

"Patience and I didn't see any on our way here."

"You cut along home like a good lad," said Mr Trick.

"I want to see those tracks for myself. I'll be right back." Before his father could protest, he had gone out the door.

"Stubborn as a mule," Mr Trick said to Papa. "Or his mother," he added.

The door opened and Mama struggled in with an armful of Indian bread root that Mrs Trick had pressed upon her. She put her load down on the stump-table, which was back in its original position. "Have a cup of loosestrife tea," she said.

"Don't mind if I do," said Mr Trick.

Sam came in with a puzzled frown on his face.

"Well, lad," said Mr Trick, "are you satisfied? Avery and I are going to set off now. I want you to look after your mother. We may be out overnight."

"I saw them, Father, but I don't like them. I don't know what it is, but something's wrong. They don't look like deer tracks."

"Rubbish, boy, of course they're deer tracks. Your old father knows a thing or two as well as your precious Indians. We're leaving now." He drained his cup of tea and rose to leave. "All that learning's gone to his head," he whispered loudly to Mama. "Turned his brain, I shouldn't wonder. Not deer tracks, my foot."

Before daybreak the next morning Miles slipped out of

the house. As he suspected, Sam was outside waiting, sitting on a pile of ropes.

"I thought you'd never wake up," he said. "We have to work fast. Those deer tracks. I didn't like them yesterday and I looked them over again just now. They're not real tracks. Someone made them and made them very well."

"Who?" said Miles.

"The only person I can think of is Grimble. He's lured our fathers away. Most likely he'll get them lost, then double back here himself."

"Will we be able to fix things in time?" said Miles, heading for the woodpile.

"Only just. Grimble will want to lead our fathers well away before he turns back. We probably have the day—if we're lucky."

They worked until breakfast cutting small stakes. After breakfast Patience helped them as they drove them into the ground in two straight lines. The stakes looked like double fences bordering a wide path to the front door. They told Mama that they were making a walk like the one in Quince Alley.

"I don't know what your father will say when he knows you've been out, Miles. But I think you're nearly better and the sun will do you good. I'm glad to see you playing once more."

"Playing!" Miles whispered when Mama went back into the house. "If she only knew." They had decided not to tell her until the last minute. "'Twould take an age to calm her down," said Miles.

"There's no time for that," said Sam.

They worked all day, half expecting Grimble to stride into the clearing and demand his treasure. When they were finished, Patience filled a kettle Sam had brought along with him and left it by the chimney-stack, with the ropes. Then she slumped beside the two boys, who lay sprawled in front of the hut.

"That's that, then," said Sam. "We're ready."

"He can come any time," said Miles, stroking Reynard.

"Not before we've all had a sleep," said Sam. "He'd make mincemeat out of us now. I'm for home."

"Aren't you going to tell the Mississagys?" Miles asked.

"I forgot. Yes, I'll go to them now." He was off.

It seemed much lonelier and darker after Sam had left. The great shadows of the trees crept across the clearing like hints of Grimble.

"I won't sleep a wink," said Patience. But it was Miles who sat all night listening in the darkness for a sound that never came.

Early in the morning, before they were properly awake, there was a knock at the door and they heard Sam's voice, low and urgent, outside.

"What is going on?" said Mama. "What a terrible time to come calling, Sam Trick."

"Mrs Avery, I heard from the Mississagys that Grimble is on his way here. My mother wants you all to come to our house until my father and Mr Avery return. It will be much safer there."

Mama was about to protest, but the expression on Sam's face convinced her that he was serious. "Very well," she said. "Children, get your things. We'll do as Sam says."

Miles took Sam outside. "What good will it do if we all go?" he asked. "How can we catch Grimble if we're at your place?"

"Never mind," said Sam. "I'll think of something. We

can't tell your mother. She would let Grimble take his treasure, so long as you were safe.''

All four set off across the clearing and down the trail. When they reached the Tricks' house Mrs Trick was waiting.

"Sam tells me that rogue is back. Well, we'll wait here and he won't bother us.'' She laid an axe near the table, which was set for breakfast.

"An axe, Maggie Trick?'' Mama said, astonished. "Surely you wouldn't use an axe on him?''

"That Grimble stands like a mighty oak,'' said Mrs Trick, "and an axe is just the thing to stop him—though our husbands would be better. Sam and Miles, go and find your fathers.''

"Yes,'' Miles said eagerly before his mother could protest. "Let's go, Sam.''

Sam glanced at Patience and sped out the door with Miles behind him.

"Do you think we'll be in time?'' Miles asked Sam as they moved quickly through the woods back to the Averys' house.

"I hope so. We'll soon find out. But no more talk.''

When they came close to the edge of the clearing, they hid behind a big rock and waited.

The morning passed slowly. The sun lit the clearing and all was still except for the angry yapping of Barnaby and Reynard inside the house. A bird cried in the distance and Hodge answered it.

Then the moment they had prepared for arrived. A bush on the opposite side of the clearing parted and the long shadow of Malachi Grimble fell across the grass and tree stumps. It almost reached their hiding-place; they pressed themselves against the rock.

Grimble moved cautiously towards the house, pausing to sniff the air and listen. Once he looked over to the rock in the bushes where they lay. Sam held his breath and Miles closed his eyes tight. In the hut the cubs yapped and Grimble turned. With a last suspicious look outside, he entered the house and closed the door. From inside there came a howl from one of the cubs, then it screamed with pain and there was silence.

The two boys ran to the hut carrying several ropes they had hidden behind the rock the day before. First they tied a rope across the doorway about eight inches off the ground.

"Faster!" panted Sam. They could hear the scraping sound of the stump being dragged across the floor. Miles ran to the chimney-stack, picked up the kettle of water that Patience had left, and quickly climbed to the top of the roof.

"Now?" he hissed at Sam.

Sam nodded his head. Miles poured the water down the chimney and jumped to the ground.

From inside came an uproar of coughing and bellowing. Then they heard a scrambling sound as Grimble struggled to recover his loot in the suffocating darkness.

Outside the boys waited on either side of the door. Suddenly it was wrenched open. Rubbing his eyes, and coughing and choking, the giant plunged forward, tripped over the rope, and crashed to the ground on top of his box, which fell under him.

The moment he fell Sam and Miles worked on Grimble, who lay stunned and winded. They tied ropes to his ankles and to the stakes in the ground. They tied more ropes from stake to stake across his back. Rope after rope they pulled tight.

Suddenly Grimble realized what was happening. He

could not move his legs or his body. He was being tied down by dwarfs with a hundred ropes! His great arms reached out and he snapped off stakes as though they were twigs.

Sam ran toward Grimble's head with a small horn box in his hand.

Grimble glared at him. "I'll tear you to pieces!" he roared.

Sam threw the contents of Mr Trick's box of snuff into his face and jumped clear. Grimble sneezed and beat the ground and sneezed until he lay exhausted.

Meanwhile Sam and Miles completed the job of fastening him to the ground. They tied more ropes to this hands and arms and attached them to stakes and tree stumps. They finished by tying a noose around his neck. "In case he still wants to fight," said Sam. Then they sat down and admired their handiwork. But the silence disturbed Miles.

"The cubs!" he exclaimed.

They felt their way into the smoke-filled hut, calling the cubs' names, fearful of what they might find. They heard a whimper and one bedraggled little fox crept out from under the bed. A moment later the other cub scurried after his brother. Miles and Sam picked them up and ran out of the hut.

"Dratted smoke," said Miles, rubbing the tears from his eyes.

"You did it! It worked!" The shout startled them.

Mama, Patience, and Mrs Trick advanced towards them from the woods. Mrs Trick was armed with the axe, Mama carried a potato masher.

"I had to tell them!" Patience said excitedly.

"You didn't think we could stay away, did you, Sammy?" said Mrs Trick. "Patience here has been all agog to join in the fight."

"Attacked and robbed by as vicious a gang of thieves as ever I saw," groaned Grimble, squinting up at Mrs Trick.

She shook her axe at him. "Not another word out of you, Malachi Grimble!"

Mama, after a horrified stare at the tethered giant, had gone into the house. She came out again hurriedly. "What a shambles he has made of it. James will be furious."

"It's *my* hut," rumbled Grimble.

"I think he will like what we found, Mrs Avery," said Sam. He led her to the wooden box that lay beside the prisoner and lifted the lid. The jewels blazed in the sunlight.

"It's a fortune!" said Mama.

"It's mine!" Grimble wheezed.

"The forest will be well rid of you," said Mrs Trick, picking out a ruby brooch and holding it against her shawl.

"This pinching winter may yet turn prosperous for the Tricks and the Averys," Mama said happily.

"Thanks to the children," said Mrs Trick.

"Now we can truly think of finding Honor again. James can start by going to Quebec."

"I'll ask him to bring Simon a box of snuff," said Mrs Trick.

Grimble moaned.

18

The Thieving Magpie

Miles and Sam took turns standing over Grimble as he lay staked out on the ground. He was so securely bound that a guard was not really necessary, but Miles said that in the army you always had someone guard a prisoner. They could hardly believe they had actually made Grimble powerless, and yet there he was, unable to move—but entirely capable of talking.

"Never heard of such a thing in all me life," he grumbled loudly whenever Miles or Sam came within earshot. "*Me*, Malachi Grimble, the terror of Lower Canada and New England too, captured by a gaggle o' mewling infants!" He glared so menacingly at Patience that she fled.

Mrs Trick rushed out at the sound of his bellowing. "That's enough o' that, Grimble!" she said sharply. "A body can't hear herself think with you screeching and carrying on." She stuffed a piece of sacking into his open mouth and bound it in with a kerchief, but not before he tried to bite her.

"For shame!" She bridled indignantly. "I wouldn't have thought that even of you, you thieving wretch."

"Mgmnf!" Grimble retorted.

After supper they decided to move him across the clearing and tie him to a big pine tree. They kept him tied and dragged him slowly while Mrs Trick stood over him with her axe, threatening to knock him into the next world if he tried any pranks.

It grew dark. "We can't watch him through the night," said Sam. "We'll have to barricade ourselves inside the hut in case he escapes. I hope the ropes hold."

Miles decided to mount guard outside, wrapped in a blanket, while the others slept. But he was exhausted and soon fell asleep himself.

He was awakened by a shout. Grimble was still tied to the tree, but he had spat out the gag and was bellowing at him. "I'm turning to ice, you scoundrels! Wake up, you pup! Murderers!"

The others rushed out when they saw Grimble sitting on the frozen ground, his hair white with frost. Mama and Mrs Trick felt sorry for him and hurried to make hot gruel.

"Put the blanket over him, Sam," said Mrs Trick. "He may be a thieving rogue, but he's a man for all that, and we can do better than make him catch pneumonia."

"You miserable devils," said Grimble. "Rub my legs and feet before I get frostbite. I've been in better jails than this one, I can tell you. One thing you have to say for being whipped, at least it gets your circulation going."

Mrs Trick popped a large spoonful of herb medicine into Grimble's mouth. He swallowed it, coughed, and as he opened his mouth to protest she popped in another spoonful.

Slowly a smile spread across Grimble's face. "Ah, there's a lady that knows her cures," he said. Much to the children's surprise, he begged for the rest of the mixture.

"There's nothing like spruce beer, punkin molasses, and water to put heart in a man," said Mrs Trick complacently.

Then Patience had the task of feeding Grimble hot gruel. She was still afraid of him, even though he was tied hand and foot, but she felt sorry for him too.

"How many people have you murdered?" she asked.

"I'm no murderer," he said. "I've broken a few heads in my time, but I've never murdered anyone. Now if you want to see a murderer, just look in a mirror."

"What do you mean?"

"What do you think's going to happen to Grimble when they get him back to Cataraqui? They'll string me up, that's what they'll do." He looked at her piercingly. Then he seemed to forget about his black future. "Keep the gruel coming there, missy."

"What are you, then?" Patience asked.

"A Gentleman—" answered Grimble, pausing to slurp more gruel "—Thief. That's my profession. And some day I'll be a Gentleman-Thief with a mansion full of my treasures. You saw my modest collection—all quality stuff that is. Not much yet, but a good start. Only now I'll have to start over again, thanks to you young 'uns."

"Will they really hang you?" asked Patience.

"If they don't shoot me first."

The morning passed. The Averys and the Tricks cleaned the smoked-out hut and Grimble slept in the warm spring sun. There was a shout from down the trail and soon Mr Trick and Papa came into sight, singing and carrying a large deer on a pole between them. They marched into the clearing and set the carcass down.

"Venison for a king's supper!" called Mr Trick. He saw Grimble and stopped in amazement.

"Sam and I captured him," said Miles. "It was Sam's idea. He said that if the Lilliputians could capture Gulliver, then we could capture Grimble."

As they walked over to the hut, Miles described the struggle to capture Grimble.

"My snuff!" said Simon Trick. His eyebrows shot up. "You used *all* my snuff?"

When they got inside, the boys slid the stump across the floor and revealed the hole.

"But look at the treasure!" Patience cried.

"The fortune of a Nabob!" Papa exclaimed when he caught sight of it.

"Of a thieving magpie!" sniffed Mrs Trick.

Mama said: "When I think of all the people that bandit has robbed, I wonder that I let Patience feed him gruel."

"With his part of the reward," said Mr Trick, "Sam can bury himself in fusty books up to his chin. What will you do, Miles? Buy yourself a musket and practise your soldiery?"

"I'd like to use it to look for Honor," Miles answered.

"Well spoken," said Papa. "But reward or no reward, I must put in the crops or we will have no grain, and you can't eat emeralds. Sam, I want to make you a present of *Gulliver's Travels*, since you used it so well. Now, let's roast the venison and celebrate."

"That reminds me," Sam said. "Those were false deer tracks you followed. Where did you shoot that animal?"

"True enough, Sammy," his father replied. "We soon

discovered that. But the false tracks crossed some real ones. As we were on the hunt for deer, we were not going to return without one. So you see, a false trail is sometimes better than none at all. Now, Sam, go and tell your friends the Mississagys that you've got a prisoner. Maybe they'll take you to Cataraqui to report his capture.''

19

Alf's Visit

"*Yo-Hah!*" said Musinigon, his black eyes glinting with pleasure. "*Keen-etam!*" He passed a wooden bowl to Miles, who sat beside Sam in the clearing. The Mississagys had just arrived to inspect Grimble.

"What did he say?" said Miles, looking inside the bowl. It contained seven plum-stones. One side of each stone was burnt black; the other had been left its natural colour.

"He said 'You go first!' You toss the stones in the air. If they land light side up it counts for you, and the black sides count for me. Whoever wins after three tosses goes to Cataraqui with Musinigon to report Grimble's capture."

Sam's blue eyes glittered like Musinigon's. He had long since caught the Mississagys's passion for gambling.

Miles tossed the stones and caught them. There was a chorus of "*Wa Wa Wa*" from the Indians and they gathered excitedly around Musinigon as he counted the four whites and three blacks.

"Now it's my turn," said Sam. "The whites still count for you." He flipped and caught the stones.

"*Wa Wa Wa.*"

Miles held his breath and again they counted four whites and three blacks.

"Now, Musinigon," said Sam, passing him the bowl. "The last throw is his."

"I can't help but win," thought Miles.

Musinigon tossed the stones high in the air, and caught them in the bowl.

"*Che che che.*" The Indians stood up, laughing, and seemed to glide out of the clearing. Only Musinigon remained.

Miles looked in the bowl. It had five black stones and two white ones.

"Take care of Grimble," said Sam consolingly. "That's really the most important thing."

"Hurry back," said Miles, hiding his disappointment.

"If they weren't taking their furs in, there would be room for both of us." With that Sam waved and disappeared with Musinigon down the trail.

Shortly after Sam left, Miles heard a roll of drums from the woods and Alf marched into the clearing.

"I've come to see Grimble for meself. But I won't stay long," Alf said firmly. "If a pack of His Majesty's finest comes to pick him up, they might want to take back a missing drummer boy. I've no mind to serve under Finlay again."

Miles took him inside to show him the treasure.

"Are you really leaving us so soon?" Papa asked Alf that night at supper.

"Stay until the soldiers come in the big batteau and you'll have a ride back with Grimble," Miles suggested.

"Always the joker, mate." But Alf stayed.

The third evening of his visit, soldiers filed into the clearing, making it bright with their flaming torches. At the front of the line strode Thomas Trudgett, with Sam at his side.

Mama threw her arms around Thomas, Papa shook his hand, and Patience danced around him. Miles saw that Alf had moved back into the trees. He waved at Miles and vanished.

"Well, Miles, not a redcoat yet?" Tom teased.

"Maybe sooner than you think." Miles stopped suddenly when he saw the last soldier to reach the clearing. It was Finlay: "Why did you bring that rogue, Tom?"

"We'll talk about that as soon as we go inside. Finlay, set up camp over there."

"Camp can wait a bit, sir. Read 'em your orders!" Finlay's face was wet with sweat, and the light of the torches turned him into a uniformed gnome.

"Away, Corporal, or I'll send you to keep the wolves company!" Trudgett's cold voice convinced Finlay, who went off and started shouting at the men.

Once they were inside, Miles said: "Only bad news could make Finlay smile. What are your orders, Tom?"

"The bad is not disastrous, so let me first tell you the good news. Your sister and relatives are safe and well in Quebec."

Mama laughed and cried, Papa shook Trudgett's hand again, and Patience and Miles sat dazed.

Trudgett continued. "A friend of mine from Oswego, Harry Nuthall, met them in Quebec and remembered them well because of their tragic story."

"Not one of the children—" Mama faltered.

"No," said Tom. "That is not it. Harry learned that they had escaped from Albany when their house was attacked by the mob. They reached New York safely and sailed for

Quebec, where Dr Vanderpflug set up practice. They were anxious to discover the fate of you Averys, and after many vain inquiries they were told that Captain Avery had been killed in battle and that you and the children had perished and your house was destroyed.''

"Poor Honor!" said Mama. "What a shock for her."

"Harry said she refused to believe that you were dead, but she's a sad girl."

"I can't wait to see her face when she hears we're all alive," said Patience. "Papa, may I go with you to Quebec? Can we leave right away?"

Before Papa could answer, Tom said: "You can't reach Quebec in time." He looked down at his mud-splattered boots in embarrassment. "They plan to leave for England on the first ship of the year. It sails in less than a week."

"But how long does it take to reach Quebec?" Mama asked impatiently.

"It would take about ten days, Abby," Papa said in a flat, tired voice. "But I think Tom has more to tell us. Otherwise he would be part way to Quebec himself by now—would you not, Tom?"

"Indeed I would, sir. 'Twas only by chance I heard the story three days ago. I tried to leave for Quebec immediately, but Castlevane heard the story too and he hasn't forgotten how we made him look a fool over the parole paper. He is in command while Major Ross is upcountry again, and he ordered me to make a full and immediate inventory of the supplies at the fort. I refused and he had me arrested for insubordination. When Sam arrived with word of Grimble's capture and the recovery of Grimble's loot, Castlevane saw an opportunity for more malevolent sport and perhaps some ill-gotten gains as well. He ordered me to bring this squad of soldiers to escort Grimble to the fort. And while I watch Grimble, Finlay watches me."

"What a vile scoundrel he is!" Papa bit so hard on his pipe that the stem snapped. Angrily he threw it in the fire.

"That isn't quite all," said Trudgett. "He ordered me to bring you in for further questioning on the old charge of desertion."

"But why raise that again? He must know that I wrote Colonel Allen asking him to write directly to Major Ross. I'm surprised that word has not yet come from Colonel Allen confirming my innocence."

"Well it hasn't," said Trudgett. "And Castlevane doesn't care. He is due to go to England. He will simply announce that you are under suspicion of desertion and therefore cannot lay claim to the reward for Grimble, and then he will no doubt get hold of it somehow. Before your evidence arrives, he will be safe in England."

"Oh, James!" Mama was beginning to cry. "I can't bear these trials any longer. I—"

"Don't cry, Mama," Miles said quickly. "Castlevane hasn't won yet. Don't forget, Honor is safe in Quebec."

"But how can we stop her from leaving?" Papa said. "Could I go now, Tom? Miles and I could both paddle."

"Castlevane would like you to try that," said Trudgett. "If the troops didn't kill you, the river would. It's roaring with spring water."

"Don't try it, James—please," said Mama. "We would be foolish not to be patient a while longer. Miles is right, the good far outweighs the bad. I'm very grateful to you, Tom, for all you have done and tried to do. Let me get you some food. You must be weary from the trip."

Miles and Sam went outside while Tom ate supper.

"Could we get to Quebec, Sam?" asked Miles.

"No. Only a Mississagy would get there in less than a week, and he might well drown trying."

"Let's talk to Alf about this. He has a sharp brain in that foxy head of his. If anyone can outwit Finlay and Castlevane, he can."

They went into the woods where Alf had vanished and Sam gave a low whistle. Alf appeared immediately and they all sat down behind a large rock.

"Well Miles, what news?"

When Miles had finished his story, Alf said: "Wait here."

He left them talking in the evening shadows and crept over to Grimble's pine tree. The soldiers gathered round their fire at the far side of the clearing were noisily eating their supper.

"Mean lot," said Alf. "I wouldn't be surprised if they finished you off before you got anywhere near Cataraqui."

"Thanks for the good cheer," said Grimble.

"I'm thinking of leaving soon myself," said Alf. "I have to be in Quebec in five days."

"Then you should have left last week," said Grimble. "I know the water like a brother, and even if the hounds of hell were after me I couldn't make it in five days."

"Could you make it in six days?" asked Alf.

"With the devil on my tail I would," said Grimble.

"Then it's a bargain," said Alf. He shook Grimble's hand even though it was tied to the tree.

"What do you mean?"

"Six days, you said. Done."

"You're mad!"

"You want to hang?"

"Do pigs fly?"

"Agreed, then," said Alf. "I'll be back when they're all asleep."

As Alf returned to his rock, he saw Trudgett leaving the house to inspect the soldiers' camp.

"I may be putting my head in a noose," he said to Miles and Sam, who sat gloomily contemplating Finlay berating the men, "but I want a quiet word with Tom out here. Can you manage it?"

"I will," said Miles. He walked over to Trudgett, talked earnestly to him for a moment, and then went on into the house after Sam.

Trudgett glanced at the soldiers, who were now singing loudly around the fire. One of them was playing a fiddle. Finlay sat gnawing a bone like a large angry rat.

Trudgett walked casually towards the big rock, sat down, and began to light his pipe. "Well, Alf," he said quietly, concentrating on his pipe, "what are you up to now, my deserting hero?"

"I'm not one to tell tales out of school," said Alf from behind the rock, "but one good turn deserves another."

"I've heard of your tales Alf. I've no need of lies tonight." Tom smoked and gazed at the stars as Alf talked quickly behind him.

Miles was wakened in the middle of the night by someone pulling very gently on his ear. A shadowy figure moved towards the door. He rose silently and followed.

The dark forms of the sleeping soldiers looked like stunted tree trunks as they lay sprawled around the smouldering fire outside. Miles crouched against the side of the hut as part of a charred log fell with a crash to the ground. One of the soldiers stirred and muttered a sleepy curse.

Miles waited and looked cautiously around. At first he couldn't see anything, but then he saw a branch moving beside Grimble. He crept into the trees and made his way towards it.

Alf was leaning against Grimble's tree. "That's not bad at all, but you'll have to move a little faster, lad," he said in a whisper.

Miles had no time to ask or say anything before Alf reached over and cut Grimble's bonds. Grimble flexed his huge hands and arms. Then he grabbed Alf's knife and disappeared into the trees.

"What did you do that for?" Miles hissed at Alf, who signalled for silence.

A minute or two later Grimble could be seen working at the base of the chimney, poking into the earth with the knife. Then he vanished.

Alf looked at Miles. "Now I've done it," he said. "He's off!"

They stood there, uncertain what to do, when a voice behind them said: "Never put all your loot in one spot, lad." Grimble had reappeared carrying a leather pouch in his hand. "Your friends can have the baubles, I'll take the gold!" He handed Alf his knife. "Now let's see how fast you can travel."

"I'm off to Quebec with Grimble," Alf said to Miles. "Do you want to come?"

"Do I? But how—?"

"No questions. We're leaving now." Alf slipped into the darkness of the woods at Grimble's heels and Miles followed.

20

The Rapids

They ran after Grimble, who led them across country to an inlet, where a birchbark canoe was hidden by the water's edge.

"Hop in," Grimble said hospitably. "Now then, chum," he said to Alf, "what's this imp doing here? I thought we were off to Quebec on our own."

"He wants to find his sister."

"A likely story. He'll turn us in at the end." Grimble glowered at Miles, who said hastily: "I won't, I promise I only want to find Honor."

"All aboard, then. We have a trip to make."

Grimble slid the canoe off the sand into the lake, jumped in himself, put on a red woollen cap, and seized a paddle. His strokes were smooth and strong and the canoe split the calm water like an arrow.

Miles was peering into the darkness ahead when a roar from behind almost made him fall overboard.

"Ah, this is the life!" shouted Grimble. "No hangman's

rope for me!'' He began to sing a voyageur song, then broke off. ''Give us a hand there, you sons of devils!'' he bellowed. ''You work your passage on Grimble's boat.''

Miles and Alf inexpertly took turns with the spare paddle and soon fell into Grimble's rhythm.

Late in the morning they passed Cataraqui and threaded their way like a needle through hundreds of green islands, some no bigger than a batteau.

''Mille Isles,'' said Grimble when Miles questioned him. ''But there's no time for gawking at scenery.'' He grinned through his beard. ''Rapids lies ahead—a pack of 'em. And we're going to shoot 'em! I'll take us through the first set— they're not so bad, and I can do it alone—but once we reach the Long Sault, 'twill take all three of us to stay afloat.'' He snickered at the sight of Alf's alarmed face.

They came to the first rapids. Even before the foaming waters came into sight, Miles could hear the din.

''And these are the easy ones,'' he thought.

Alf sat curled in a dismal heap in the straw on the floor of the canoe. ''Why did I ever leave the army?'' he moaned. ''I could be in a nice safe dry stable right now. Oh!'' The first billow of water struck the canoe.

''Here we go!'' shrieked Grimble, who was in high spirits. ''Hang on, landlubbers!'' He pulled his red cap over his ears and began to guide the bucking canoe through the turbulent waters. The canoe flashed between rocks like a silver fish attacked by the fury of the torrent.

Miles enjoyed the dizzying sensation. At times the canoe was turned around altogether or became almost buried under sudden bursts of water. He loved the roar of the water and the sting of the spray.

Alf lay at the bottom of the canoe with eyes closed until the roar died away. Then he raised his head. "Not many more of those, I hope," he said.

"Dozens," said Grimble unkindly. "And they're not far away, neither. The Long Sault's a fair treat, it is." He handed his paddle to Alf. "You blackguards keep her moving while I rest."

Alf took up the paddle and shakily tried to match Miles' rhythmic stroke. When he found it, he grew more cheerful and began humming to himself.

Miles was soaked; soggy straw and pools of water lay on the floor of the canoe—but he was totally happy. The sun dried his hair and warmed his shirt. A fish leaped from the water and fell back with a splash. White clouds foamed above like rapids in the sky. His arms, no longer aching, felt pleasantly tired.

"Alf?"

"What is it?"

"Will father go to jail when he gets to Cataraqui?"

"Not a chance. Before I went with the Mississagys I hung around Cataraqui and learned a thing or two. A certain British officer and his sneak have been stealing settlers' supplies. They store them in a warehouse in Barriefield and smuggle them over to an American pedlar. A nice little game, and Cataraqui has made a tidy profit from it."

"Why didn't you tell?" said Miles.

"I got nothing against stealing, have I? Anyway I did tell Tom. Now Castlevane will get the cell reserved for Grimble."

"Did Tom believe you?"

"Of course he believed me. He's not like some folks who think that liars can't tell the truth ever. What will you do after we get to Quebec and find your sister?"

"*If* we get there in time to find her," Miles said.

"Don't worry. Grimble will get us there. What will you do then?"

"I want to join the army. I might even go to England with my uncle and join the army there, and be an officer in the Dragoons. If I get a chance to go to England, I'll go."

"What makes you think you'd like it, Pikonekwe?"

At the sound of his Indian name, Miles flushed. "I've wanted it all my life."

"But are you sure you still wants it? Look about. You like this Canada with its waters and winds and trees. British officers don't paddle and sing and snowshoe and hunt when they feels like it. It's all spit and polish and yessir, nosir, three bags full sir."

"I want to be a dragoon," said Miles dourly.

"Time to eat now," said Grimble. "I'll catch us some fish." He beached the canoe while Miles and Alf stretched and groaned after their long hours of paddling.

When they had eaten, the boys stretched out to sleep, but Grimble soon prodded them. "No time to sleep now! We're off down the Long Sault. Up you get!" He herded them back into the canoe. "We cross Lake St Francis tonight," he boomed. "I've got some nice rapids in store for you tomorrow! Château du Lac, The Cedars, The Cascades—"

"I don't want to hear no more about it," Alf said grumpily.

Next day, late in the afternoon, they hurtled over the last set of rapids at Lachine. Paddling furiously they burst into quiet waters and drifted with the current. Grimble let the boys paddle while he made himself a smoke with Alf's tobacco.

"Look, Miles, over there! Ahead on your left!"

In the distance Miles saw church spires glittering in the

sun, and the buildings of a town inside a ruined wall. Behind it crouched a mountain, freshly green with the leaves of spring.

"Montreal!" said Grimble with satisfaction. "Ah, many's the merchant I've robbed there. Get some sleep now, me hearties. Four more days and we'll be in Quebec. I wonder how all me old cronies are faring at the Black Bear—if they've not been strung up by the heels, that is."

"Have you been to Quebec too, then?" asked Miles. "You seem to have visited many places."

"Grimble's been everywhere and stolen everything," he said. "And never been whipped through the streets yet neither," he added proudly.

21

Honor Found

The north shore of the river became higher and higher. The forest came closer to the river. Then the northern bank turned into bare slate cliffs. The river narrowed and an enormous bluff jutted out into it. They rounded it and entered a busy harbour.

"There she is!" Grimble bellowed. "Six days, I said, and I keeps me bargains." He waved his paddle. "Quebec!"

Even Alf fell silent. There were two towns: one on top of the cliff and one below on the river shore. Grey towers and buildings spilled down the rock between them. Sea-gulls flew through a tangled thicket of masts. Among the ships of all sizes were two brigs, the *Albemarle* and the *Aurora*, resting majestically in the basin, their sails furled like folded wings. A canoe, paddled by a man in a cap similar to Grimble's, streaked through the water like a hunted minnow.

Miles saw Grimble eyeing the whitewashed houses that lined the shore like a row of sentinels.

"Merchant's houses," Grimble said, licking his lips

greedily. As if piled on top of each other, the densely packed tin-roofed buildings rose on up the rock, which was crowned above by spires and ramparts. Grimble paddled the canoe closer to the wharf and Miles could see a narrow street twisting up the side of the rock.

"Hop ashore, lads. This here's the Cul de Sac where the likes of *us* lands," Grimble said. He slid past the nose of an oncoming flatboat and paddled the canoe onto the muddy shore.

Miles leaped out and promptly collapsed in a sea of mud.

"Your sister's going to think you're a mudfish." Alf scrubbed the foul mud from Miles' face and clothes.

"What a smell!" said Miles.

"Tide's out," Grimble told him. He lifted the canoe out of the water and pulled it up to dry land. "Quebec folks puts all their cleanings along the shore."

Miles picked his way past piles of straw, decaying fish, bones, and bottles that lay strewn in slimy heaps by the river.

"Where do I start?" he asked Grimble. He inspected the two brigs. "Will they be sailing on either of those?"

"The *Aurora* is sailing soon, but she won't be ready for near three days by the look of her. And the *Albemarle*'s just come." Grimble took off his red cap and scratched his matted hair. "I'd try the *Aurora*."

"What if we're too late?"

"Rest easy," Grimble said. "See the scraped paint on the *Albemarle*? She's had a rough passage—through ice, I shouldn't wonder. No, you get yourself aboard the *Aurora* and find out from the mate where your sister stays. They'll have a list of passengers. That's the ship, you mark my words. There's a rope ladder a-dangling there right now over the side. Alf'll take you out to it." Grimble set the canoe back in the water.

"Aren't you coming with us?" Miles asked.

"You just hop along to the brig and ask your questions, lad, but remember, don't say my name to anyone. When you have some news, meet me in that tavern." Grimble pointed to the sign of the Black Bear. "Come through to the back and ask for Gros Jean. Mind, don't get lost!"

Alf guided the canoe over to the *Aurora*.

Miles looked up at the rope ladder that dangled over his head.

"Up you go, sea-monkey," said Alf.

Miles balanced precariously on the canoe and caught the swaying ladder, almost wrenching out his arm. Hanging on with only one hand, he swung backwards and forwards for a full minute until he managed to catch the ladder with the other hand and clamber up. He came over the side, waved to Alf, and went in search of the mate.

He saw a boy about his own age chewing tobacco and swabbing the deck with a mop.

"I would like to see the mate," said Miles.

The boy pointed to him silently, his jaws still working. As Miles moved aft the boy spat overboard and muttered derisively: "Mud-dubber!"

"I am not," Miles growled, unaware of the trail of his muddy footprints.

The mate stared at him. "Well?" he barked, not seeming to like what he saw.

Miles drew himself up. "I wish to inquire for Dr Vander-pflug and his family," he said, trying to sound like Papa. "And Miss Honor Avery. Are they taking passage on your ship?"

"That's as may be," said the mate, winking at the swabber who had silently mopped up behind Miles and who stood waiting, his mop poised for another footprint.

"It's my aunt's family," said Miles, suddenly desperately homesick. "And...and my sister. They've been missing, or rather we were. Can't you tell me where they are staying and when this ship sails?"

"Don't take on, laddie," said the mate kindly. "The ship won't leave for three days yet. I'll take a look at the passenger list for ye." He disappeared below while Miles and the swabber stared at each other.

"St. Louis Street it is," said the mate, emerging from the darkness. "Near the Gate. Avast, ye scum!" he shouted at the swabber, who reluctantly went on with his swabbing.

"Thank you, sir," said Miles, anxious now to find the Black Bear and St. Louis Street.

"What news?" asked Alf after Miles had slithered down the ladder and landed gingerly in the bobbing canoe. "What kept you? I thought you'd 'listed in the merchant marine instead of the army."

"Full speed ahead," Miles said gaily. "We've nearly found her!"

They beached the canoe in the Cul de Sac and pushed their way along the crowded riverside street towards the Black Bear. Narrow shuttered windows on steep-roofed houses stared at them balefully like watchful eyes. Black-robed, bare-footed priests sauntered by, along with sailors and pipe-smoking habitants. The smell from the wharf lingered dankly in the air. A squad of soldiers marched briskly towards them just as they came to the Black Bear.

"Not again!" moaned Alf and he vanished inside.

Miles stood for a moment in the sunlight to examine the

creaking sign. "The Black Bear looks like Grimble," he thought. "I wonder if he sat for its portrait."

He pushed the door open and stepped into a babble of unfamiliar words, angry shouts, and raucous songs. The vile smell of the street was replaced by a rich blend of ale, tobacco, porter, ripe cheese, and soup. Miles was blinded after the brightness of the street. As he looked about in the murk for Alf and Grimble, he stumbled and fell on the floor.

"Use your eyes, blast you, or I'll 'ave 'em out of yer 'ead!"

Miles could see now. The room was half-full of sailors and voyageurs. The man who had shouted at him leaned forward across the table and caught him by the shoulder. He lifted him off the floor and shook him.

"You're new here," he growled. "What d'ye want?"

"Gros Jean," Miles gasped as he swung back from the great hairy arm.

The man sat him down gently. "Through there, lad. No offense meant. Just a bit miffed 'cause you banged the old leg." Miles looked down at the pegleg and up again at the bearded face. "Straight through ye go, lad, but don't tell the big 'un I laid an 'and on ye."

Miles went through a curtained doorway and into the back of the tavern where he found Grimble and Alf eating breakfast. Grimble had a tankard of ale in his hand.

"Here's our raggletailed hero," said Grimble. "Did you see a ghost?"

"I hope not," said Miles. He sat down and looked hungrily at the freshly baked loaf of bread and the steaming bowls of soup on the table. "Can I have some? I feel as if I hadn't eaten anything except fish for most of my life."

"Of course, lad!" Grimble reached out, twitched the

curtain, and the man with the pegleg hobbled in. "More soup, more bread, and more ale," ordered Grimble curtly.

"Yes, Jean." The man looked pleadingly at Miles, and, moving sideways like a crab, vanished and soon reappeared with the food.

"Eat up, then," commanded Grimble. "Alf told me your news. St. Louis' where the nobs live and they won't be up yet. I'll take ye there as soon as I've had another ale."

Miles ate hungrily. "The mate said they are sailing in three days. You did it, Grimble. My family owes you its thanks."

"Pay 'em to Alf, here," said Grimble. "It was his bargain I kept."

"Honour among thieves," laughed Alf.

Miles choked over his ale.

"Come along, lads, we'll finish the trip now," said Grimble, banging down his tankard.

The spring sun dazzled their eyes as they left the Black Bear. They turned from the river and walked along Champlain Street to climb the steps that led up to Mountain Hill and Upper Town. As they climbed higher they left the smells and gloomy houses behind. Now the air was sweet. They passed splendid churches, handsome stone mansions, orchards, and gardens. A group of nuns hurried by and disappeared into one of the grey buildings.

Church bells tolled. They stepped back as a funeral procession laboured slowly by. Priests chanted prayers and small boys in white robes and black caps carried candles beside the bier. A dog pulling a small cart trotted past them.

"Close your mouth, you country bumpkin," said Alf, poking Miles in the ribs. Ahead of them Miles saw a platoon of soldiers and beyond that the walls and a gate.

"There's your gate," said Grimble. "This is where we leave you. If you need any further help, ask for us at the Black Bear, but you'd better come alone."

"Wait!" cried Miles, but they were off. He stood on the corner for a long time looking after them.

"I never thought I'd miss a pair of thieves," he thought.

He looked at the neat houses that lined the street without a break, handsome tall houses with gleaming steps and freshly painted shutters.

"Who are you looking for?" An old woman had stopped beside him. She had a loaf of bread under one arm, a covered basket on the other.

"Doctor Vanderpflug." Miles wondered why the napkin in the basket was moving.

"Four doors along."

A small dog poked its head out and stared at him with bright eyes.

Miles thanked the old woman and hurried on. A brass plate shone against the big black door. He raised the knocker—it was shaped like a fox—and banged it down.

"Yes?" A tall skinny girl looked down at him suspiciously.

"I want to see Doctor Vanderpflug," said Miles.

"I'm sorry, the Doctor is not home," said the girl, and started to close the door.

Miles pressed his hand against the door to hold it open. "I didn't come this far to be turned away!" he said fiercely. The girl pushed harder and Miles lost his temper. He pushed the door open with all his might and the maid screamed.

"What is this commotion, Martha?" A tall woman appeared behind her.

"This young mudlark tried to break in, Ma'am."

Miles didn't know how to begin. He thought the woman must be his Aunt Sally—she reminded him of Mama—but he wasn't sure.

A boy about his own age appeared beside the woman, and then a younger girl, then another smaller girl, then another boy. Miles watched the growing number of faces staring at him.

"If Philip will bring his rabbits," he said, "and Meg her cat, and Nicholas his snakes, then the whole Vanderpflug clan can examine this mudlark!"

There was a little shriek. "It's Miles!" A tall fair-haired girl broke out of the group, threw herself at Miles, and hugged him. Then she stepped back for a second and stared at him. "Miles, is it really you behind all that sludge? Yes—yes, it is!" She hugged him again.

Miles, unaccustomed to having a girl—even a sister—hug and kiss him, could only say: "It's me, Honor. I'm glad I found you."

"Oh, Miles! I knew the rebels wouldn't get you! Papa, Mama...They are with you? They're all right? And Patience—?"

"Fit as fiddles, every one. We have a farm near Cataraqui."

"Oh, Miles!" Honor hugged him again.

His cousins had by this time surrounded Miles, who was still standing in front of the door. Aunt Sally intervened. "Come in out of the cold," she called. "Leave the boy room to breathe. You're clucking like a hen, Honor. Come in, come in."

They all trooped indoors, Honor hanging on to Miles, as Aunt Sally continued talking. "I am so glad to see you, dear. What a surprise! Where did you say your mother was? Is she in the wilderness? Poor Abigail. Have you eaten?''

"Now *you* are clucking, Aunt," said Honor. "Shall I take Miles to my room and I'll share with Meggie?" The little girl squeezed her cat and beamed at the prospect. "Miles can catch his breath and then tell us everything."

"Give him some clean clothes too. Philip's should fit well enough."

Honor propelled him past elegant rooms, up the carpeted stairs, and into her large sunny bedroom. After he had washed and changed into Philip's old shirt and breeches, she sat him down in an armchair by the window and curled herself up on the window-seat. "Tell me again," she said. "Everyone is safe?"

"They are all well and happy. Except for one thing—they want you."

"Mama is really living in the woods? She thought Philadelphia was the frontier." Honor sat up on the window-seat and looked out over the street, trying to imagine her mother fighting off wolves.

"Is it very wild?"

"Papa kills a bear or a wolf every morning before breakfast, but it isn't so bad. Rattlesnakes do lie about all over the clearing, but they're sleepy in the mornings. I've only been bitten twice."

"Oh!" Honor drew in her breath. Then she saw that Miles was grinning. "Don't tease me like that!" She threw a cushion at him.

"Don't start fighting already," said Aunt Sally from the door.

The children were clustered around her. "I'd like to be a settler," said Caroline. "Wouldn't you, Nicky?"

"Not me," said Nicholas, who was short and plump.

"I'm off to school in England and when I'm old enough I'll join the army and be a cavalry officer."

After the noisy group at the door had disappeared, Honor said to Miles: "That was your ambition in Philadelphia."

He flushed beneath his tanned skin. "Yes," he said. "That's the life for me."

"Are you still going to join the army?"

"Well—yes, I think so. If I can get to England."

He didn't feel like talking about his future. Instead he told Honor about the Tricks and Alf and Grimble, even though he kept wanting to dwell on his canoe trip to Quebec and shooting the rapids. But this did not interest Honor. She could not hear enough about the family's life in the woods and had to be assured over and over that no one had succumbed to the cold or been taken off by Indians.

"Did you see any Indians?" she asked.

"See them? I lived with them."

"Were you captured?" Honor was horrified.

"No. I stayed with them in their camp. Sam Trick took me—they are his friends. Now they're mine. There is nothing frightening about them. When I go back—"

"Oh, Miles! You're not going to England after all!"

"Well. . ." Miles hesitated. "Maybe, maybe not. But Musinigon—he's Sam's friend and mine too—he can teach me things like living in the woods and hunting the way the Indians hunt, and tracking animals. You don't know these Indians. They can see things we can't see. They told me you'd be found."

"What do you mean?"

"One night we asked the Great Turtle—that's their spirit who tells them things—if you were safe and if we would see you again."

"What did it say?"

"It said you would return when trees walked, liars tell the truth, and there is honour among thieves."

"What did it mean?"

"Well we moved a tree stump—I suppose that means it walked. Alf told the truth for once. And Alf and Grimble—they're thieves, and proud of it—they made a bargain and kept it. That's honourable. And it's because of them I'm here."

"I wish I could meet them. Oh, Miles, I want to leave Quebec and see Mama and Papa and the farm."

"You'll see where we found the treasure."

Miles produced the response he expected. "A treasure? You found a treasure?"

"Right in our house. But we can't keep it."

"What did you do with it?"

"I suppose they've taken it to Cataraqui by now. But we'll get a reward."

Miles began to describe how he had stolen away in the night with Alf and Grimble without telling Papa.

Suddenly there seemed to be too much to explain. He could no longer keep his eyes open.

Honor let him fall asleep in the chair.

22

Miles Makes His Choice

"Children!" Miles awoke to the sound of Aunt Sally's voice. "It's time to change for dinner. Colonel Seawright and Captain Hamilton are coming and they will help us to celebrate Miles' arrival."

Honor was standing over him. "I'll get Philip's good clothes for you," said Honor.

"Can't I wear these?" Miles said sleepily.

Honor smiled at him. "Young officers-to-be change for dinner," she said gently.

So Miles did the best he could with his hair, and put on Philip's frilled shirt and breeches. "Stupid clothes," he muttered as he struggled with the buttons.

Honor laughed when she returned. "Now you look like a fine young gentleman—except for your feet."

"Do I have to wear shoes?"

"Yes."

"Just wait until you get to Cataraqui," he said, eyeing Honor's elaborate gown and the trinkets in her hair. "It will be deerskins for you."

"I won't mind. I'd leave this minute if I could."

They went downstairs together to the dining-room, but Miles stopped shyly in the doorway until Honor pushed him inside.

Silk curtains shielded the windows; candles lit a long table glittering with crystal and heavy silver.

Uncle Stephen saw them and called Miles over to meet the officers he was talking to. He was a tall raw-boned man with red hair and arms that seemed slightly too long.

"Miles, my boy, you're astonishingly like your father. But you're more man than boy after what you've been through." He put a hand affectionately on his shoulder.

"Colonel Seawright and Captain Hamilton, may I present my nephew, Miles Avery, from Cataraqui?"

"So you are the ruination of my voyage to England," said the Colonel, beaming at him. "I had been looking forward to the company of your aunt and uncle on board ship. Now I'll have to play chess with Captain Hamilton and he hates chess."

"We shall stay in Quebec," Uncle Stephen explained to Miles. "We were going to England only to discover word of your family. Sally hopes we can persuade your father to bring you all to live in Quebec."

Miles looked at him in surprise.

"Meanwhile," Uncle Stephen continued, "I know that your parents will be anxious for your safety and I suspect that Honor would like to leave tomorrow, if not tonight. So I have made arrangements for you both to sail tomorrow for Montreal."

"Thank you, Uncle Stephen," said Honor. She stretched up to kiss her uncle's leathery cheek.

"Father—" began Nicholas.

"Don't worry, Nick," said Uncle Stephen. "You will still go to England. The army needs you."

"Everyone seems to be taken care of but us." Captain Hamilton hung his head in mock despair. "*I* had hoped to enjoy Miss Honor's company on the long voyage. Now I shall have to play chess."

Honor blushed and everyone laughed.

"Please be seated," said Aunt Sally. She motioned to Martha who scuttled back and forth with a variety of dishes whose very names Miles had forgotten.

"The river brought us another traveller today," Captain Hamilton told the company. "An informer brought word as I left the barracks that an infamous thief is in town, one Malachi Grimble. You wouldn't know him, Doctor, but he plagued us mightily a few years ago, and it will give me great pleasure to hang the rascal."

"Have you caught him?" asked Honor.

"No, but he will be at his old haunt, the Black Bear. We'll get him there after midnight tonight."

"It will take half the army to capture him," said the colonel, fingering his mustache. "He's a powerful rogue."

Miles looked to see if Honor would say something, but she was listening politely to the captain.

The officers and Uncle Stephen began discussing military affairs.

"You have learned your history well, Miles," said the colonel when Miles argued with him about the battle of Culloden and won his point.

"I learned my battles well, but not much history," said Miles.

"Now you sound like Papa," said Honor.

"What else is there in history except for plague and famine?" asked the captain.

"If James Avery were here he would lecture us for an hour on the Greeks," said Aunt Sally, ringing for Martha to take away the plates.

"Now *there* were soldiers for you," said Captain Hamilton. "Alexander the Great and those Spartan fellows. If the Loyalists had had a tenth of their discipline we would be sitting in Boston tonight, not leaving for England."

"What do you mean?" said Miles. The captain glanced at him, surprised by his tone.

"Don't be upset, lad," he said lightly. "You must know that if the Loyalists had been trustworthy and given us a little support instead of constantly going home to tend their crops, we should never have lost those inglorious skirmishes the rebels call battles. We couldn't depend on them."

"And if that fool Howe had attacked Washington in Valley Forge instead of sitting comfortably in Philadelphia all winter in '78, the Loyalists would have some crops to tend now!"

"An excellent meal, Mrs Vanderpflug," interrupted the colonel, stretching comfortably, "and a most enjoyable discussion." He smiled affably at Miles, but his eyes were stern. "Your aunt tells me you have long cherished the desire to serve in His Majesty's army, Miles. Let me give you a word of advice—you must learn not to be so free with your opinions."

Colonel Seawright beckoned to Nicholas, who had listened respectfully to his every word during dinner.

"Fetch me a pipe, will you, my boy?"

"Yes, sir!" Nicholas jumped to his feet and ran to the pipe-rack.

"Yes sir, no sir, three bags full, sir," Miles muttered.

"What did you say?" asked Honor, who had overheard him.

"I was just remembering a friend." Miles turned to Aunt Sally. "Please excuse me, Aunt. I feel very tired now. May I go to my room?"

"Of course, Miles." She smiled fondly at him. "Honor, you may be excused too. You must still have much to say to each other."

Once safely in Honor's room, Miles scrambled back into his deerskins. Like Sam, he always carried a rope, and he began to tie it around the bedpost of the massive bed.

"I'm going to warn Grimble."

"I thought so," said Honor. "How can I help?"

"Stay here and don't let anyone in. When you hear a sea-gull cry, see if it's me and let down the rope. I won't be long. Grimble and Alf aren't much for farewells."

He slid down the rope, waved at Honor's anxious face in the window, and set off across town. It had been raining and the wet streets of Upper Town glistened when the moon shone through the drifting clouds. Half sliding, half running, he plunged down Mountain Hill. He couldn't find the stairs they had climbed earlier, but came upon another set that disappeared into the darkness. He lost his footing and fell several steps. He groaned, picked himself up, and walked more cautiously to the bottom.

"I hope they're here," he thought when he finally came to the Black Bear. He pushed open the door and looked in on a wild scene of singing and drinking. A sailor lay slumped on the table, his face in a puddle of ale; two men who looked like pirates argued fiercely in a corner; and a scrawny pig rooted for food on the refuse-strewn floor. Miles made his way through the brawling crowd to the back of the tavern and pushed aside the curtain.

Alf and Grimble sat at a battered table with three villain-ous-looking men playing cards.

"How are you, Miles lad?" said Alf cheerfully. "Tired of high life already or did they turf you out?"

"What is it, lad?" said Grimble.

"You'll have to hurry," said Miles. "Someone told the army you're here. They're coming for you tonight!"

Grimble picked up his winnings and looked around at the others.

"Not us, Grimble," one of them gibbered, backing away from the table. "Would we be here if we had ratted on you?"

"You find out who did," said Grimble roughly. "Alf and me got to move along now, but you find out. I'll be back one day." He turned to Miles. "You're taking a risk here, lad. Be off, now. Grimble thanks you. He won't forget."

"Don't join the army until we get out of the way," said Alf, pulling on his coat.

"I'm not joining at all," said Miles. "I'm going home."

"Thought you might," Alf said. "Say hello to Patience for me."

They were in the street in front of the Black Bear. "You never thought I'd go to England, did you?" Miles said.

"Not once you'd been your own master. Well, goodbye, Pikonekwe."

"Goodbye," said Miles. "Good luck." He watched Alf disappear with Grimble into the shadows of the street, and then climbed back up the hill.

As Miles emerged from Lower Town the storm began

again. Lightning illuminated the river below in flashes; the hills and spires were bathed in an unearthly yellow glow. Rolling kettle-drums of thunder played a duet with the sharp beat of the rain on tin roofs.

The house on St. Louis Street was in darkness. He gave a low sea-gull cry and a rope flopped down from a window above.

"I got there in time," he told Honor after he had climbed into the room. "What happened here?"

"I said you were asleep and had asked not to be disturbed. Colonel Seawright and the captain left just after you did. I heard them say they were going straight to the barracks for a platoon of men and then on to the Black Bear. What if they had caught you there?"

"They didn't, Miss Accomplice."

Honor paused at the door. "You've grown up since I last saw you, but you're still my little brother." She smiled and suddenly looked like the Honor he remembered. "So wash your face, hang up your clothes and you'll find a nightshirt at the foot of the bed. You need to rest before we leave for the wilderness in the morning."

She left before he could reply.

Miles looked at the huge bed with its puffed up pillows, white sheets and soft mattress. He pulled off a blanket, put it on the floor, rolled himself up in it and with a grin of satisfaction watched the lightning split the sky. He thought of Alf and Grimble, out in the darkness.

"They won't catch you now," he said. "They won't catch any of us."

Afterword

Although the Averys' adventures are imaginary, their way of life is based on historical facts. Because we live in Kingston, we decided to bring the family here, overland from Philadelphia. So one of us went off to the library every day to learn about that splendid American colonial city. The other went to work. Somebody had to earn a living.

For the next two years, in between writing, plotting, listening to bouncy recorder music, and fighting with the editor—and each other—we paid a visit to Williamsburg, Virginia, and the living museum of Annapolis, Maryland, and followed the little yellow feet of the Freedom Trail in Revolutionary Boston. We drew maps, pestered patient historians, and made notes, many notes on Games, Books, Costume, Ballads, Food, Language. . . .

Apart from general history books, we read eighteenth-century diaries, newspapers, letters written by court ladies, soldiers and admirals, the memoirs both bleak and cheerful of aged settlers. Most of our sources were in the Douglas Library at Queen's University, Kingston, Ontario, and are not easily available, but four of our favourites might be found in a public library.

There was the great Swedish naturalist Pehr Kalm who visited North America in 1748–51. He travelled everywhere, describing with equal enthusiasm flowers, bugs, buildings, fences, and the skittish young ladies of Quebec who leave "their mothers to do all the work of the house." He tells of the habits of black snakes and of the Recollets, the Barefooted Monks who "do not torment their brains with much learning."

Almost as useful were the recollections of Madam von Riedesel, wife of a German general, who followed her husband to Canada with three small daughters, aged four, two, and ten weeks. She then followed him to the battle of Saratoga where everyone was captured and taken prisoner to Boston. Her lively journal and letters are full of gossip and invaluable details of domestic life in eighteenth-century North America.

It seemed only reasonable to use the information from that delightful plagiarist Thomas Anburey. And there was the immense hunger-provoking Diary of Parson Woodforde (1740–1803) who lived quietly in his Norfolk parish and ate steadily throughout half the century. On 11 December 1784, he and a few friends tucked into a dinner of "a boiled Leg of Mutton with Capers, a Couple of Chicken rosted and a Tongue, a Norfolk plain batter Pudding, Tripe, Tarts and some blamange with 4 sorts of Cheese." For Supper they contented themselves with "some Oysters, a wild Duck rosted, Potatoes rosted, and some cold Chicken &c."

And who were they, these Loyalists, who came from all parts of the United States?

They were not wealthy and cultivated English aristocrats, but farmers, bricklayers, hatters, and innkeepers. They were Hessian soldiers from Europe, Scots Highlanders, Irish, Dutch. They were Indians, leaving their lands in the Mohawk Valley, fields filled with corn, pumpkins, and beans, and fruit trees. They were black soldiers, escaping, they hoped, to freedom.

There *were* men of property too: lawyers, merchants, doctors, clergymen, but most of these went to the West Indies or England where they worked to achieve high position and repayment for their losses.

The Loyalists in the newly formed United States suffered in many ways for their loyalty to the Crown. They were fined and taxed into poverty. Families were split, brother against brother, husband against wife. George Washington's mother was a Tory, so was Benjamin Franklin's son.

Many were imprisoned, horsewhipped, dragged through pools, ridden out of town on a rail. The dreaded tarring and feathering (it was actually pine pitch, which is stickier) was so horrific that being given a warning blob of cold tar and a handful of feathers was enough to make one leave by the next boat.

People had different reasons for being Loyalists. Not all of them were keen believers in the divine right of kings or thought that everything the British government did was just. Many believed in the American dream of freedom and liberty for all men but were dismayed by the violence of the mob or the idea of armed rebellion. Others agreed with the toast: "My country, may she always be right; but right or wrong, my country."

After the signing of the final peace treaty in 1783 there was no way for most of these so-called traitors to live on in the new republic. They had no rights. They couldn't vote or hold political office, buy land, or collect their debts. And so they began to leave the United States in great numbers.

Many had left already. The first batch went with the army to Halifax after the evacuation of Boston in 1776. A gleeful Patriot described the scene: "all is uproar and confusion;

carts, trucks, wheelbarrows, handbarrows, coaches, chaises, all driving as if the very devil was after them.''

"The crazy flotilla" pitched and tossed for six days in the turbulent March waves before reaching Halifax. In one cabin thirty seven people—''men, women, and children; servants, masters, and mistresses—were obliged to pig together on the floor, there being no berths.''

Thousands more fled from New York in 1783 and settled in Nova Scotia (which then included New Brunswick) and on the Island of St. John (Prince Edward Island).

Meanwhile other Loyalists were streaming across the border into temporary settlements of huts and tents in Sorel and Machiche. From there they were sent to the Gaspé and upriver by batteau to Upper Canada. Others came to Fort Niagara, or like the Averys slipped across the border wherever they could.

Flung into the wilderness penniless and often in rags, the Loyalists found their new life hard. Diaries and letters are full of despair and complaint: "I am totally discouraged"; "I am sick of this province"; "All our golden promises are vanished in smoke. We were taught to believe this place was not barren and foggy as had been represented, but we find it ten times worse." Nova Scotia was nicknamed Nova Scarcity.

But the government did offer substantial support, especially in Upper Canada. That unjustly-forgotten Swiss general, Governor Haldimand, often ignored the orders of his London masters and helped these unruly new settlers as best he could. They were given clothes for three years, assorted tools, axes and handsaws, fire-locks for the pigeon and wild-fowl season, and seeds to sow crops. Most important of all, they were given land.

Once settled on their forest property, the Loyalists faced many trials: loneliness, sickness, wild animals. There were no churches, schools, stores, roads. After the crops failed in 1787, came the Hungry Year when people were reduced to eating buds and roots and tree bark. One family subsisted for two weeks on beech leaves; an old couple survived on pigeons who obligingly allowed themselves to be caught. Later one settler recalled, "The Bay of Quinté was covered with Ducks of which we could obtain any quantity from the Indians. As to fish, they could be had by fishing with a scoup. I have often speared large Salmon with a pitchfork. Now and then provisions ran very scant, but there being plenty of Bull frogs we fared sumptuously. This was the time of the famine I think in 1788, we were obliged [to] dig up our potatoes after planting them to eat."

But eventually most of the Loyalists prospered. They were one of many waves of people who have populated Canada. Their influence, good and bad, has been strong.

Further Reading

If you want to read more about the Loyalists and their times, visit your local library. You may find these books helpful. Those marked * are written for children.

Anbury, Thomas. *With Burgoyne from Quebec*. Edited by Sydney Jackman. Toronto: Macmillan, 1963.

*Bacon, Martha. *Sophia Scrooby Preserved*. Boston and Toronto: Little, Brown, and Company, 1968.

Brooke, Frances. *The History of Emily Montague*. Toronto: McClelland & Stewart, 1961.

Brown, Marvin L. Jr. ed. *Baroness von Riedesel and the American Revolution*. Chapel Hill: University of North Carolina Press, 1965.

Caniff, William. *The Settlement of Upper Canada*. Belleville: Mika, 1970.

Conant, Thomas. *Upper Canada Sketches*. Toronto: William Briggs, 1898.

Crary, Catherine S., ed. *The Price of Loyalty: Tory Writings from the Revolutionary Era*. Toronto: McGraw-Hill, 1973.

Earle, Alice Morse. *Child Life in Colonial Days*. New York: Macmillan, 1927.

*Forbes, Esther. *Johnny Tremain: A Novel for Old and Young*. Boston: Houghton and Mifflin, 1943.

*Fryer, Mary Beacock. *Caleb Seaman: A Loyalist*. Toronto: Ginn, 1970.

_____ *Escape: Adventures of a Loyalist Family*. Toronto: Dundurn Press, 1982.

_____ *John Walden Myers: Loyalist Spy*. Toronto: Dundurn Press, 1983.

Guillet, Edwin C. *Pioneer Travel in Upper Canada*. Toronto: University of Toronto Press, 1966.

Hunter, Robert. *Quebec to Carolina in 1764 to 1786*. San Marino: Huntington Library, 1943.

Kirby, William. *Annals of Niagara*. Niagara Falls: Lundy's Lane Historical Society, 1972.

*Loeper, John G. *Going to School in 1776*. New York: Atheneum, 1973.

Moore, Frank. *A Diary of the American Revolution*. New York: Washington Square Press, 1967.

Nelson, W.H. *The American Tory*. Toronto: Oxford University Press, 1961.

Preston, Richard A., ed. *Kingston Before the War of 1812*. Toronto: The Champlain Society, 1959.

*Raddall, Thomas. *His Majesty's Yankees*. New York: Doubleday, 1942.

Sabine, Lorenzo. *The American Loyalists*. Boston: Little, Brown, 1847.

Talman, J.J., ed. *Loyalist Narratives of Upper Canada*. Toronto: Champlain Society, 1948.

Van Tyne, Claude. *The Loyalists in the American Revolution*. New York: Macmillan, 1902.

Wallace, William Stewart. *The United Empire Loyalists: A Chronicle of the Great Migration*. Toronto: Glasgow Brook & Company, 1914.